THE EMPEROR OF PARIS

CS RICHARDSON's first novel, *The End of the Alphabet*, was an international bestseller published in fourteen countries and eleven languages. Winner of the Commonwealth Writers' Prize for Best First Book (Canada and the Caribbean), it was named on four Best of the Year lists and was adapted for radio by BBC Radio 4. Richardson is also an accomplished and award-winning book designer. He lives and works in Toronto, Canada.

From the international reviews of *The Emperor of Paris*:

'A rare gem of a book. The prose is considered, yet light and engaging. The plot is careful, ephemeral and tightly wound. The book picks you up, then spins you along. Sharply, sweetly unforgettable' *January Magazine*

'Stunning... the grace and humanity of Richardson's storytelling is the stuff of classics... Romantics, book lovers, day dreamers beware — CS Richardson is out to steal your heart' *Telegraph Journal*

'The novel shimmers with the heightened clarity of a dream... the reader will be swept up, and will read with anxious, bated breath' *National Post*

'A feast for the senses, and a deeply touching account of love, loss and destiny' *Vancouver Star*

D1052322

Also by CS Richardson

The End of the Alphabet

the
Emperor
of
Paris

CS Richardson

Portobello
BOOKS

First published as an ebook by Portobello Books 2012
Hardback edition published 2013
This paperback edition published 2014

Portobello Books
12 Addison Avenue
London
W11 4QR
UK

Originally published in Canada in 2012 by Doubleday Canada, a division of
Random House of Canada Limited.

A CIP catalogue record is available from the British Library

9 8 7 6 5 4 3 2 1

ISBN 978 1 84627 113 7

Text design: Kelly Hill

Offset by Avon DataSet, Bidford on Avon, Warwickshire

Printed and bound by CPI Group (UK) Ltd, Croydon, CR0 4YY

www.portobellobooks.com

For Hannah and Alexander

The observer is a prince enjoying his incognito wherever he goes. The lover of life makes the whole world into his family, just as the lover of the fair sex creates his from all the lovely women he has found, from those that could not be found, and those who are impossible to find, just as the picture-lover lives in an enchanted world of dreams painted on canvas.

CHARLES BAUDELAIRE,
The Painter of Modern Life, 1863

For the gossips of the bakery it becomes irresistible: the wisps of smoke up their noses, the voices under their windows, the footfalls of curiosity on the move. They are the first to arrive, these busybodies, shading their meddlesome eyes and comparing their hare-brained theories.

Mark this day, someone says. We are witnessing the devil's work. Only Satan would burn a library.

It is providence, comes a retort. God's design unveiled to us mortals.

Either way, says a third, it is a cruel deity. A cruel one indeed, dooming a good man to such a horrible fate.

The bakery's more level-headed regulars appear. Some to stand rooted to the cobbles in disbelief, others to pace back and forth, frantic now to do anything that might help their bread man. An old fellow elbows through the mob and pulls at the bakery's blue doors. The locks hold firm, his thick spectacles knocked askew with the effort. Three or four boys scatter in search of buckets; a fifth runs off to call the fire brigade. An elderly woman shouts the address after him.

Heads are scratched and hands are wrung. In the summer heat handkerchiefs are pulled from pockets and sleeves; foreheads wiped, eyes dabbed, mouths covered. A bout of coughing, then someone asks if anyone has seen the baker.

Out wandering, I should think. Sunday after all.

A fortunate day then, and all the better that our man isn't here. Imagine watching your life going up in flames. Luckier still he isn't cinders himself.

And where will all this luck be, I ask you, when he arrives home to nothing? After all his collecting, all those armloads of books? It will break the man's heart.

A cruel one indeed.

The crowd becomes a small fidgeting sea in front of the bakery, each face turned to a sky the colour of pearls.

They watch in silence, holding their children close, praying the brigade is not delayed in traffic. Above them the baker's apartment disappears.

Smouldering flakes begin to blossom in the heavy air, sliding over slumped shoulders, resting for a moment on shoe tops, dying tiny shrivelled deaths in the street. There are glimpses here and there: a sentence, a phrase, a doomed word drifts by. Among the singed white bits are shards of red leathers and frayed blue cloths, the curled and blackened edges of marbled papers, melted strands of silk ribbon, everything spinning slowly to the ground.

On a July morning in the eighth district of Paris, it begins to snow.

In his time the baker's father had been a celebrated man, though he held no official title. A sign had never hung on the bakery's doors: BEHOLD EMILE NOTRE-DAME, THINNEST BAKER IN ALL PARIS! Nor had the thought occurred to him to take advantage by placing a notice in the shop window: AND YET HOW STOUT HIS BREADS!

This matter of thinness was the source of endless debate among the gossips queuing for their daily loaves. Some claimed that Monsieur might as well be invisible. With those legs our dear Emile is more than

4

worthy of the honour. Others were certain that among the countless bakers in the city there must be scrawnier candidates. Someone would then suggest that it was not Monsieur's stature that had made him worthy. Our man is the very model of service, they would say, to his craft and to us. He rises at ungodly hours, makes us good breads in bad weathers, and hands them over with a smile and a story. I could not care less if the fellow were made of twigs.

In the end all agreed it was a marvel—considering the temptations of butters and yeasts and eggs—that any baker anywhere in France might be as slender.

There was never a discussion regarding the size of the baker's wife. A woman of Italian descent and feverish religion, Madame Immacolata Notre-Dame was in her other aspects generously round. Only her head was small: a gracious sphere covered with black hair drawn to the nape of her neck, her high-collared blouses making her head appear all the smaller. No one addressed her as Immacolata. To all she was simply, piously, Madame; and her Emile was their Monsieur.

The bakery occupied the ground floor of a narrow flatiron building known throughout the neighbour-hood as the cake-slice. As far back as anyone could remember the letters above its windows, in their carved wooden flourishes, had spelled out:

BOULA GERIE NOTRE-DAME

the N having long since vanished.

All who visited the bakery agreed the signage was as charming as the squeezed triangle of building that housed the bakery and the thin and thick of its husband-and-wife proprietors. Yet there were demands that Monsieur make repairs. The more excitable gossips insisted that tourists might loiter, having made a wrong turn somewhere and found themselves unable to decipher *boula* and *gerie*. You will have these poor souls, monsieur, fumbling for a guess that the broken word means *cathedral*. Which will only make them anxious as they wonder if they are in the right district at all. Then there will be the emptying of luggage in search of phrase books and maps. And then, monsieur, you will have the unthinkable: underclothes and stockings and goodness knows what else thrown all over the street.

To calm these worries, Monsieur would concoct a story concerning the N's disappearance. He might begin by suggesting that Napoleon himself had taken it. The little general would spring to life in the figure of Monsieur: climbing a wobbling ladder, straining to reach the prized letter, prying stubborn nailheads with his fingers. With each telling the location of the missing consonant changed. It once turned up in Les Invalides, glued with wallpaper paste to the lid of the great man's tomb. Monsieur leaped from the last invisible rung and took a deep bow.

You are welcome to retrieve it, my friends.

The bakery's location in a building named for a pastry confection was an irony lost on no one. For centuries there had been an order to the world, a natural division of gastronomic labours. Bakers worked their dough, pastry men fussed with their marzipan. Each kept to his own, begrudging enough if he found himself walking past the other's shop. To feed your family, you were off to the boulangerie. Weakness for a macaron meant a trip to the patisserie and be quick about it. It was a sensible order: everyone knew to visit a fruit seller when looking for a squash was foolishness; dogs and cats in the same litter meant the end of civilization.

Yet these were modern times, the gossips were quick to remind. We must change as the world does, monsieur.

All too easily for Monsieur's liking. Bread was the stuff of life, for him the stuff of generations: the Notre-Dames had been bakers as far back as there had been

7

Notre-Dames. We have fed kings and washwomen, he would boast. Our breads have soothed teething babies and started revolutions. I ask you: would you sop up your grandmother's cassoulet with a handful of apricot jam? I should hope not.

No. Monsieur would not betray a guild older than the Pyramids by fooling with custards and icings. Others might offer their éclairs alongside their country rolls—heaven forbid in the same display case—but such fraternity was not for him. You can stuff me with mousse, he would grumble, before I start ladling meringue into a pie and serve up a month's worth of indigestion for my trouble.

Each customer remained just as loyal to this creed, though on occasion, should Monsieur take a break from the ovens and join his wife upstairs, a quiet comment about raspberry tarts might slip out of a gossip's mouth.

The walls of the bakery were decorated with allegories: a woman with blushing cheeks held a bouquet of wheat sheaves to her bosom; a laughing baker snorted plumes of aroma from a glowing oven; winged infants hoisted trays of pains au chocolat, delivering breakfast to the gods. A glass case stretched the length of the shop, displayed ranks of braided loaves, croissants nestled like lovers, curve within curve, boules scored with the initials N-D, baguettes in two lengths. Next to the case sat the till, an iron beast requiring a well-swung fist to open the drawer. Wicker baskets were everywhere, in chronic danger of being knocked over, and overflowing with varieties of sourdough and rye, wheat rolls with sweet hidden raisins, and Monsieur's gently herbed brioche.

Above the door to the cellar and its ovens hung a calendar advertising a peerless and heavenly beer. The calendar featured a portrait of the Virgin Herself, in shades of pink and purple, her eyeballs spinning in ecstasy, beams of orange light bursting from her head. A golden bottle, sweating in the holy warmth, hovered in the clouds above her.

With the day's last customer served and gone, Monsieur and Madame would climb the stairs to their apartment in the top of the cake-slice. Morning after dark morning, down to fire the ovens, polish the marble, upright the baskets. Evening after evening, up to home and bed.

The Notre-Dame household was solid underfoot but slightly out of level, a boat nestled at low tide. The lounge and kitchen were one room, furnished with a pair of arm-worn chairs. The dining table had come from a café near the cake-slice, a wedding gift from the proprietor. The bathroom floor sloped its own way into a bedroom where Monsieur would cheerfully move the bed should Madame wish to open the armoire drawer. The attic, reached by a circular staircase that rose inexplicably from the centre of the main room, was a space of rough-hewn beams and mouse-hole corners. If Monsieur leaned out the attic window at a particular angle and shooed away the ever-present gathering of pigeons, he might enjoy a view of the chimney pipes of the district.

Honoré, saint of bakers, stared from prayer cards tacked throughout the apartment. An Italian bible, swollen with strips of paper marking Madame's preferred verses, was the extent of the Notre-Dame library.

Someone new to the Boulangerie Notre-Dame, standing at the distant end of the morning queue, could enjoy a few distractions till their turn came. Having finally stepped inside, they might admire the bakery's painted tiles. Or watch the stock of baguettes dwindle ahead of them and worry whether there would be any left when they reached the counter. Or turn their attention to Monsieur and Madame bustling behind the display case. An unlikely pair, the newcomer might wonder, tapping the shoulder next in line and asking how this curiously thin baker and his hefty missus had met. Heads would turn, throats would clear, and the hive of the bakery would come to a halt.

A gossip would say it was strawberry. Another would reply that no, it was raspberry.

As you wish, but I am sure it happened near the river.

In the park, you mean.

Monsieur might slide his arm around Madame's waist. As I recall we were on the boulevard, he would say.

Well then, Monsieur, it was most certainly a Saturday evening.

Sunday afternoon, Madame would reply, offering a hint of a smile as she spoke, and leaning her head against her husband's shoulder. The debaters would pay no attention as they circled the newcomer.

You must visualize our baker here, strolling along on his day of rest, his head—

in the clouds as usual, conjuring another story when—

he passes a pastry shop and—

averts his eyes as any proper baker would and—

fails to notice the young beauty emerging from the shop.

Madame would look at her husband. I was eating a tart, wasn't I?

Monsieur would kiss his wife's cheek. A treat, he would say. After mass.

There would be the inevitable collision: Monsieur ending up in the gutter, Madame with most of the tart smeared across her face. He leaped to his feet, ready for a yelling match, and turned to meet his foe. There she stood adjusting her shawl, cleaning custard from her dress, blushing and cursing a streak in Italian. She was the most beautiful creature he had ever seen. He smoothed his hair and rummaged through his pockets for a handkerchief. Once he had found it, he paused as she nodded her permission. He wiped a dribble of raspberry ganache from the corner of her mouth. She never stopped staring into his shining grey eyes.

So there it is, someone would conclude. I knew it was raspberry.

The important thing, Monsieur would add, was that it was red.

On that dessert Emile and Immacolata built their life together, though none who knew them were bold enough to remark that such happiness had begun, of all places, outside a pastry shop.

There were the Sunday afternoons in a small café near the Boulangerie Notre-Dame: the same outside table no matter the season, her mother chaperoning a few tables away. Emile would arrive with a copy of the day's illustrated newspaper tucked under his arm, present the front page with a flourish and weave a tale concerning its illustration. Immacolata would roll her eyes or gasp at the proper moments, not caring that her handsome baker never began his stories by reading the headline.

A front page once featured the unveiling of an enormous marble statue in a far-off museum. Emile spoke of the marble in his own bakery, explaining in a deep voice and with many a dramatic pause that its slabs and tiles had travelled across a sea—teeming with sharks and mermaids, he said—all the way from the quarries of Sicily.

But there is no marble in Sicily, Immacolata said. They have a volcano. There they mould their statues out of molten lava.

But I am sure my marble came from Italy. Certain of it—by boat—across the sea—teeming—

Then your marble began its journey in Tuscany. Like me.

And the sharks—the mermaids?

Immacolata glanced at her mother a few tables away, then placed her hand on Emile's.

Still swimming as far as I know. I was only little, but I remember watching them through the railing as we sailed away.

———

The spring of 1901 saw Emile and Immacolata married in an alcove chapel of the Church of Saint-Augustin. There followed a small celebration in the bakery. Emile baked the choux buns for the pièce montée himself, admitting to no one that a week earlier—under cover of a late-night stroll—he had consorted with a pastry man in the ninth to produce the cream filling for the buns.

A few customers had arranged for a duo of cello and violin. Naturally the gossips were first in the queue for a dance with the bride.

On Sunday mornings Madame would drape a shawl over her head, touch the palm of her hand to the nearest Honoré and set off to church. In leaner years she might have been seen shuffling to mass on her knees, and once, as joyful as a martyr, she likewise made the pilgrimage to Chartres by scuffing up and down the aisle on the train from Montparnasse station. Through each mass she prayed to Gabriel, hands clenched, knuckles white, begging for the gift of children.

When his wife had left for services, Monsieur would dress in his one black suit, step out of his clogs and into his Sunday shoes, comb his unruly hair, button his only collar and descend to the bakery. After polishing the counter with his sleeve, Monsieur would step outside, inhale a morning free of flour dust, and place his bony bottom on the curb. Only then did he lean his back against the bakery's blue doors and scrutinize the pictures in his illustrated newspaper.

On an afternoon in December of 1907, with a north wind stabbing at the bakery windows, Madame received an answer to her prayers. As though a lover's breath had wafted across the nape of her neck. Standing behind the counter, she held a hand against her cheek, then crossed herself. She caught her fingers in the closing drawer of the till.

Next? she said, perhaps too loudly.

Through the following summer Madame seemed to double in size. The morning of the eighth of August found her in hard labour in the cellar of the bakery, splayed on the same table where, were it any other Saturday, Monsieur should have been scoring his second lot of baguettes. In spite of the early hour, the day promised to be the hottest of the summer.

Ovens at full heat, rising loaves overflowing their pans, Madame's ankles balanced on Monsieur's shoulders, customers filling the shop upstairs and fretting about whether anyone had gone to fetch a doctor, the gossips among them suggesting hot water and cold towels and opening or closing as many windows as possible, all combined to make circumstances in the bakery more uncomfortable than anyone could have imagined.

By midday a quiet cry was heard coming from the cellar. Everyone in the shop took turns grinning and slapping each other on the back, then left in search of champagne and the good crystal. Monsieur placed his newborn son in a bowl of proofing dough. He mopped his wife's brow and smoothed her hair and chuckled at his own joke.

Quite a loaf you've baked, my love.

Everything in Madame's head came loose and spun into blackness. Half naked, bloated and torn for anyone to see, she panicked at the sudden emptiness inside her. At feeling nothing for the trembling thing beside her in the bowl, its pink fists wavering above the rim. She waited for the joy, the relief, the excitement, the peace.

Monsieur whispered that the boy would need a name.

Madame looked away, her thoughts tumbling in a thousand directions. She had worn her knees raw in devotion. She had been so correct, so careful, full to bursting with faith in Gabriel's kindness. She could not remember a day when she had not dreamed of motherhood. She had wanted this child since she herself had been a child. Now the shivers of fear would not stop. Was this Gabriel's reward for her selfishness? To give a gift only to turn His back and deny the want of it? Madame stared at her husband, tears pooling in her unblinking eyes, flowing down her face and welling on the marble under her.

I am trying so hard, she said.

Monsieur forced a smile. Rest now, my love. I will think of something.

The boy spent his first night swaddled in the drawer of his parents' armoire. He slept, as day-olds do, peaceful and unaware.

The following morning Monsieur's newspaper depicted the moment after a train had collided with an elephant. The surprised animal hurtled through the air as the engineer poked his head from the engine's cab, the man's cheeks puffed and pink as he blew on his whistle. The headline told of A STRANGE RAILWAY ACCIDENT IN SIAM!!

Another Sunday and Monsieur might have managed a fantastical story, one he could not wait to tell his wife when she returned from mass. Animals, birds, mythical creatures: these were his specialties. The elephant might transform into a mad runaway from an African travelling zoo. Or become a gift to the mayor of Paris, delayed on the outskirts of the city, from the

Maharaj of Calcutta. He would invite Madame to join him on the bakery step, then transform into a fidgety public official rattling his watch to see if it still worked, or a grand and puffy Indian prince, bowing with apologies and trying to keep his turban on his head.

But a new father's mind is full of other dreams and other worries. Monsieur barely noticed the newspaper's date: *8.8.08.*

Monsieur ran through the bakery and up the stairs to the top of the cake-slice. He could hear the fits and gasps of his wailing son. He found his wife in the bedroom trying to nurse the infant, her face turned to the ceiling.

Octavio, he said, stretching the *ayvio* into *ahhvio* and waving the newspaper above his head. You see, my love? Eighth day, eighth month, eighth district.

Madame's eyes were swollen; her hair hung in drenched tangles.

Your son, she said.

Ours.

His wife did not reply as Monsieur left to warm a bottle of milk. Outside, the skies above the cake-slice sagged in the summer heat, threatening a downpour.

The baker makes for home, west now, his face toward the sun. He carries a bundle tied with twine, three books bound in green linen. The load knocks his shins with each stride; the rough string handle cuts into his hand. He nears the end of a well-travelled route, but on this day it holds no comfort.

It had begun like no Sunday before it. He had set out from the bakery, a head full of possibilities. A week had passed, he thought. Surely she would have found his gift. She could be there even now, at this early hour, in the gardens waiting and wondering who had left such a lovely thing behind. Would she know it was intended for her?

He had pictured her as he hurried along. She was sitting in her chair by the boat pond, loosening her scarf in the warmth of the July morning, smiling as she read. She was starting to write something. Making a note of a favourite, he was certain, the one tale in a thousand that had always been *his* favourite.

Through the morning he had tried to keep his usual pace and schedule. He had visited his favourite bookstall on the quay. Yet he had barely spoken to the proprietor, had rushed through his selections and settled on the green ones without giving them much thought. He had crossed the Pont des Arts almost at a run. He had forced himself not to look as he made his way through the Tuileries toward the boat pond.

But he had seen her empty chair. Was he behind his time, had he missed her? Or had someone else seen it, thought it forgotten, thrown it away? He had waited. The woman never appeared. Finally a groundsman began dragging the chairs strewn around the pond back to their proper places. The old fellow then picked up her chair, brushed off the dust and carried it to the trees nearby. No one had used it for some time.

———

The baker passes a café, tripping over the outstretched legs of a gentleman seated on the terrace. The man pays no attention as he juggles his newspaper, grabbing at the edges, trying to fold the paper inside out, frustrated that his arms are not long enough. He closes the paper to fold it lengthwise, one hand sliding from the top corner, the other gripping the bottom. He manages only to tangle his wrists in the middle and crease the paper the wrong way. The baker regains his footing and shuffles on.

Through a small park now. Huddled near the carousel, children surround a circus strongman, bouncing up and down as though on their own beds, their fingers stretching for invisible ceilings. The strongman holds a book in one hand. With pretended effort he hoists a chair with the other, his eyes never leaving his reading. In the chair sits a squealing girl. She waves to her friends below, their arms wrapped around the strongman's meaty legs. On the carousel, white horses pause in midgallop, waiting for their distracted riders.

The baker passes a pair of old women sitting on a bench. Each reads an identical copy of a cheap paperback. One grimaces as though stabbed through the heart and slaps her book closed. At the same moment, the other stifles a gasp with her hand, her eyes growing wide.

A December wind armed with ice and knives gathered its skirts in a northern sea. It stepped ashore near Calais, dithered before finding the Paris road, moaned its way south through thick and ancient forests, entered the town of Beauvais along the high street, paused in front of the cathedral, circled the market square, then lifted its frozen hems and slipped uninvited under the door of the town's only clothing shop.

To waft around the fat thighs of Pascal Normande, kneeling behind the door and encased like so much mince in a waistcoat embroidered with peacocks, an immaculate suit, high collar, silk tie and pearl stick pin. He ran his fingers around the frame, measuring the drafts. In such a position, his face would glow an alarming shade of pink. His plump lips tightened to a sneer.

Screw these goddamn farmers, he said.

He grunted as he got to his feet, brushed the knees of his trousers, tugged at his waistcoat, fingered his collar and peered through a frost-skimmed window to the empty square beyond.

Screw them all to hell and back.

Pascal had seen no more business this day than yesterday, or the day before, or the month past, or in the year since opening Atelier Normande. Yet in a glance he surveyed the shop, reassuring himself that all was ready. Poised, he might have said were the weather not so frigid.

Dismembered mannequins leaned against the icy walls. Shelves sagged under the weight of fabrics: bolts of browns and greens, a selection of Irish wools, rare satins, saffron cottons from the dye pots of Morocco. In the window a chorus of heads wore a collection of CHAPEAUX MERVEILLEUX!, so proclaimed the advertising card, each aeronautic brim layered in country dust. A row of ladies' footwear, their toes placed neatly in line, stood along the counter.

Behind which: Madame Céleste Normande. Forced by the temperature in the shop to abandon her code of daywear, she was wrapped in a rough blanket that would eventually produce a rash. She looked to her husband, a wisp of vapour escaping her clenched teeth.

Paris, she said.

Pascal Normande had been born in the city's twentieth district, the bastard son of a piecework dressmaker. She had doted on her boy, only to stitch herself to death in the backroom of a musty ladies' shop. The first suit he owned was the one he had worn to grieve her. He had made it himself, those dark days and nights at her elbow leaving their impression; his buttonhole work as fine a tribute as any eulogy. He promised her grave that he would be the Normande to improve the family's lot.

Céleste Renault was the daughter of a porter who had made the rounds working the finer hotels of the boulevards. As a girl she would put on her cleanest smock, tug the hem down to cover a hole in the knee of her stockings, and meet her father after his shift. She sat in his lobbies, practising grown-up postures under the potted palms, admiring the guests as they came and went. The heaps of travelling cases would bring on a fit of giggles whenever they jammed the revolving doors. On their way home, she would ask her father where the luggage had come from. The brass-riveted trunks, the leather wardrobes as tall as she was, the hatboxes decorated as though they were birthday cakes.

How much could all that hold, Papa?

A world entire, her father would say. The likes of which you and I will never see.

They grew up in the twentieth, Céleste at the top of the Belleville hill, Pascal at the bottom. Yet their paths never crossed until the World's Fair of 1900.

Tracing through the exhibit halls and pavilions, the fair's great attraction was the Moving Promenade: the guidebooks described it as A MARVEL OF AN AGE TILL NOW UNFULFILLED! The contraption consisted of wooden platforms sliding along at different speeds. At a slow and easy pace, the inner course was advertised as being for those of weak or infirm constitutions, women, young children and the clergy. The outer course moved twice as fast.

Pascal, grown into a young gentleman, stood on the outside gripping the handrail and trying to look relaxed as he moved along. Near the Russian Pavilion he passed an enormous black hat on the slower course, its brim shading the face of Céleste. Though the hat was from one or two seasons past, it was the burst of orange pheasant feathers across the crown that caught Pascal's practised eye. He knew them instantly as a bit of magic, an inexpensive trick that on the right head could distract the viewer from noticing less fashionable details of an ensemble. And he knew they had worked on him: he began shuffling backwards to stay alongside this vision. He lifted his bowler and complimented her on her dress. Céleste scanned the neatly parted hair, the athletic shoulders, the slim hips, the gleaming shoes. She offered her hand. Pascal took it and, without a moment's hesitation, Céleste stepped from the slower platform to his. Together they moved off toward the Palace of Electricity, the feathers' long tapered ends swaying with the speed.

Céleste believed, once, that her husband would do as he vowed on the day the smallest of emerald rings had finally emerged from his pocket: he, the enthusiastic Pascal, would build for her a life that would see a jewel on every finger. She, his dearest, dearest heart, would live under cloudless skies. They, the newly engaged Normandes, would stride into the twentieth century with elegance and style. They may be obliged to begin that journey outside Paris, with rents being what they were, but sooner or later the city would beg them to return.

By the evening of her first day in Beauvais, *once* had become a word for fables.

Madame Céleste tightened the blanket around her shoulders and threw Pascal his scarf and gloves. A smile as cold as her fingers creased her face.

Paris, was all she said.

Within the week the Normandes were gone, the shop's shutters left banging in the winter wind. The loss of a good tailor, like the arrival of the medieval armies that had once trod their fields to muck, the citizens of Beauvais shouldered with characteristic stoicism and dry humour. They would recall the December of 1907 as having the strangest sort of weather.

Atelier Normande reopened on the first day of the new year, unveiling its windows in a Paris back street near, though not quite near enough, the prominent fashion houses. A summer collection was presented—most notices called it quaint—petits fours were served, Pascal scurried about.

One newspaper did remark on Madame Céleste's dress. She skimmed the article, her eyes pouncing again and again:

The hostess's ensemble—a fearless stroke against convention—cascades of silk and velvet—magnificent, magnificent—dangerously exciting—supple territories at the shoulder and décolletage—the women of Paris—London—New York—will think twice about their dreary wardrobes—brava! they will shout as they rip their tired seams—rework their waists and hems—brava, Madame Céleste!

She turned to her husband. As well they should, she said.

The August skies had cleared. Pascal Normande slid a key from his vest and locked the shop, leaving the cutters, seamstresses and pressers to work through the night. A new season approached and preparation was all.

Pascal believed a client of Atelier Normande expected timeliness or they just as promptly took their business elsewhere. He conveniently forgot that his clients were not those of the great houses. They were a more practical sort, interested as much in the thickness of their billfolds as in the newness of their wardrobes. Just as conveniently he forgot how his mother had spent her nights.

He pulled his handkerchief from his sleeve and wiped his face. He cursed the wet heat sliding up from the river, along the boulevard, around the corner and through his front door. Convinced the day had been the hottest of the summer, he set off for home.

One might have missed the soggy handkerchief, the stained hatband, the flushed cheeks; such was the re-hearsed swing of Pascal's walking stick. Here was a gentleman, one could assume, overdressed for the weather but still at ease with himself and his world, wanting for nothing. For Pascal Normande was in the business of illusion.

It was an expensive business. The last francs in his Beauvais pockets had been spent moving back to the city. Every franc since went to outrageous taxes and mysterious fees. Every franc that did not pay his work-ers, or barely covered the rent on his apartments, or dripped from his wife's earlobes, every centime lever-aged or mortgaged or begged, threatened his end.

And yet. Word had it a shipment of Chinese silks sat idle and cheap on a wharf in Le Havre. Simply wire the money and an autumn line, the talk of the boulevards, would appear as though from thin air. There were rumours of a baroness planning a series of fancy dress parties for the following spring. Fold a franc into the aprons of the kitchen staff and a winter's worth of orders would materialize like aces from one's sleeve.

Pascal stepped off the pavement to allow a governess and her young charges to pass. He touched the brim of his hat. A few paces on, he stopped and looked back, his pink face brightening.

A children's collection, he thought.

With a few mothers in the client book, no shop on earth would be more magical than Atelier Normande.

At that moment Madame Céleste was at home selecting a hat for the evening's opera. *Carmen*, box eleven. Adjusting the angle of the brim and running a hand through a nest of ribbons, she rehearsed her exit from the taxi, the discreet hoist of her hems to avoid the puddles left by the afternoon's rain, her walk up the grand staircase, the curve of her necklace, her pause, her pose, her wave to an acquaintance, the turn of her feet as she stood waiting for the chair to be slid under her charmeuse bottom, the glare in her eye and the arch of her brow at the usher's flustered request: would madame be so kind as to remove her hat?

As she passed each mirror in the Normande apartments, she paused and considered her reflection. The tickets would have cost Pascal a fortune.

Her smile, she concluded, was perfection.

A one-room apartment hides in the shadows of a small courtyard. Inside a young woman paces the uneven floorboards, dressed only in her underwear: a cotton chemise, dull and shapeless with overwashing. She circles the room, stumbling over books, sidestepping memorized knotholes. She fusses over the time, rechecks the address she had written on a strip of paper. Her stomach in knots, she worries the weather will be as oppressive as yesterday's. She fills a cup from the kitchen tap. The gulped water makes her belly complain all the louder. She frets over what to wear, frets then over her fretting. From a rope strung above her bed she takes down a hanger. Her only proper dress: summer cotton, a ghost of its former rose-petal pink, the waistline long out of fashion. The sleeves, she thinks, heaven help me what if I sweat. For a cooler fit she considers shortening them or removing them altogether. She knows she could do the alterations blindfolded, the number of times she has watched others manage it.

She slips on a pair of canvas shoes. Flat-soled, broken in, comfortable for the walk. She adds her best scarf, the one with the suggestion of peacock feathers. Once a vivid swath of violets and greens, its colours faded now with time and wear. She checks in the mirror by the door, smoothing the scarf to each side of her face and throwing the ends over a shoulder. One motion, as mindless as breathing: the look, the adjustment, the toss.

The young woman picks up the parcel she will deliver, running her fingertips over the careful re-wrapping, smoothing lingering wrinkles in the paper. Satisfied no one could suspect it had been opened she takes a breath and settles her stomach. Then a flash of memory: the man in the Tuileries.

She had recognized him from the museum. He was carrying a bundle of books, which had explained the stories he told about the paintings. Her story man, she had named him.

Had she seen one of his books work its way loose from the bundle as he passed? Would he have forgotten such a beautiful thing? Impossible, she thinks. The books he was carrying that day were frayed and worn, at best second- or third-hand editions. Nothing so cared for as this one, certainly none so carefully wrapped. And if it had fallen, how would it have found its way to her chair by the pond? No, she decides. This one belongs to someone else. A child to be sure, judging by the scrawled and misspelled handwriting at the back. For a moment she imagines how anxious the young owner might be, how he might be missing his favourite stories, how upset she would be if she had misplaced one of her own books. She decides to hurry to make her delivery. It is the least I can do, she thinks, for a fellow reader. With luck I can finish the errand and return to the boat pond in time for lunch.

The young woman locks the door to her apartment. A voice calls from the darkness of the courtyard, as though her mother has waited for this moment to rise from her grave.

Are you the daughter of gypsies, child? If you insist on walking out so plainly, then remember to cover yourself. Tighten your scarf, my dear; we do not want someone staring for the wrong reason, do we?

On a crowded Geneva tram, the evening commuters looked up in annoyance, their elbows bumped, their newspapers jostled, to see someone rushing for the rear doors. They returned to their reading without a second thought. The young man stumbled into the street.

He gathered himself, slapped at the satchel slung across his chest and dug his hands into his coat pockets. Relieved he hadn't left anything behind, he turned his shoulder to a gust of wind as the tram moved off into the dusk.

He found a bench in a nearby park. A woman with a small child hurried past, both bundled against the cold. He watched them as he lowered his head into his upturned collar. The pair rounded a corner and disappeared.

He pulled off his gloves and blew on his fingers. He removed a sketching book from his satchel and laid it across his lap, gently, as though the air itself might dissolve the paper. He rummaged through his pockets for his penknife, pulled a pencil from his jacket, made one more survey of the park. He began whittling at the pencil.

Testing the point with his thumb, the young man closed his eyes and pictured his left hand hovering over a fresh page.

A hesitant line, the beginning curve of a reclining form.

Two more strokes, echoing arcs: one for the shoulders, one for the pelvic joint, drawn at opposing angles to the bodyline.

The legs. One line turning out from the hip, the other raised and bent to form a peak. Arms: the right cocked to bear the weight of the upper body, the left outstretched, resting on the knee to come. Then quick strokes, suggestions of slender fingers extending from relaxed hands.

And now the head. A simple oval: relaxed, leaning easily to one side. As though absorbed in conversation.

The young man buried his drawing hand in his armpit. He squinted at the oval, tilted his head in unison, felt the stiffness in his own neck.

He ached for anatomy. For an easel and a place amid a circle of fellow students. For a master to stand at his shoulder as he painted: offering encouragement, a gentle suggestion regarding technique, or perhaps even telling his classmates to gather round and watch a future member of the Academy at work.

The young man thought of his mother, her face pinched and worried, were she to learn of his ambitions. And his father, entering someone else's balances in a ledger, dreaming a noble life for his son.

The face. A midline vertically through the oval, for the eyes a horizontal. Two more: the line of the mouth; the tip of a nose eventually to be straight and handsome. Swipes of eraser to sharpen the jawline and hollow the cheeks. And the eyes. Deep-set, shadowed under the brow. Heavy strokes marked the crease of eyelids; fine lines became lashes. Each pupil darkened with layer on layer of lead, a tiny spot left to reflect the light.

He ached for creation. For life to somehow rise from the drawings in his sketching book. For his own energy, his own impressions to swirl and spin on a canvas. For a dream city he had tacked above his bed: postcard parks warmed with a painter's light.

The young man signed the corner of the page.

Jacob Kalb, December 1907.

A Saturday, the following August. The Paris Direct from Geneva pulled into the station twenty minutes behind schedule. The sky could hold no more: a summer rain broke in waves across the station's glass roof. The third-class carriages remained out in the weather.

Jacob Kalb, a stuffed carpetbag under his feet and his knees under his chin, hurried a last sketch of the old woman across the aisle. Since crossing into France he had managed a passable likeness of the woman's pocked cheeks, the creases around her puffy mouth. In small vignettes he had made studies of her hands and their bouquets of arthritic fingers. On the page her hair looked like lengths of wire exploding from under her hat.

The conductor assured everyone that the rain would stop at any moment; it was only a short walk into the station. Jacob checked his pockets. The money pulled from a tin under his bed, together with the address of a traveller's hotel found in an old guidebook, was still where he had put it that morning. He tucked the sketching book under his coat. The conductor touched the brim of his cap.

Welcome to Paris, monsieur. Mind the step.

Horse-drawn buses loitered outside the station; one or two automobiles chugged past. Jacob looked in the direction of what he sensed might be west, searching for a landmark, something recognizable from his bedroom wall. The rain stopped as suddenly as it had begun; already the cobblestones steamed. He pulled the guide from his pocket, tried to untangle the maze of streets.

The quintessential Parisien, the guide advised, *is known to favour walking as a mode of transport*. Jacob tightened his bootlaces, shouldered his carpetbag and stepped over a recent deposit of manure.

His mother would have found the envelope by now, propped against her most cherished possession, a photograph of a stiff and uncomfortable toddler. Jacob remembered her telling and retelling the neighbours how much the photograph had cost.

She would be reading the letter, with her usual stoic frown, stifling tears with a quiet cough, rummaging for a handkerchief. Jacob could hear her voice as though she had followed him out of the station. But why here,

Jacob? Of all the insanity. This city is no place for a boy. And who will feed you? Where will you sleep? Could you not draw your pictures back home? Your father and I could send you to Paris when you are a year or two older, if that is what you truly want.

Jacob adjusted the load across his shoulder and wished he could rewrite the letter, add something about already being older, that he would write once he was settled, that he already missed her spice cookies, that he was a man now, that she and Papa had taught him well.

He knew his father, having returned from the bank, would be for the moment silent; sitting in his dim corner, deaf to his wife's worry, wondering how to explain to his best customer that the letter drafted for his signature— You'll remember my son, sir. His apprenticeship with your firm—would no longer be needed.

The boy will be fine, my dear.

Jacob wished his father were tugging at his mother's arm as they followed him, gently pulling her back toward the station, leaving him to make his own way through the crowds along the boulevard.

He resisted the temptation to retrieve the guide-book. *And not a plodding vagrant is our native of the City of Light, but one that takes the greatest pleasure in wandering for the sake of it, with neither the assistance of map nor compass nor indeed destination of any kind.*

———

After handing the manager's wife a month's advance for an attic room and relieving himself into a trough that was the toilet two floors below, Jacob stepped over the bed and draped his damp clothes from a beam. Falling against the thin mattress, he opened his sketching book to a blank page.

8.8.08. Arrived. The Academy on Monday.

He sketched the remains of the room's wallpaper, the flaking relics of what had once been a pleasant floral pattern. Someone's notion of a touch of home for the footsore.

Through the park now, the baker waits at the curb for a lull in the traffic.

Across the roundabout a mother and her son unfold a small table. The woman carefully positions an orchid planted in an old teapot. She turns it this way and that, searching for its best aspect, facing its one bloom toward the customer. The boy leans a small sign against the pot. The baker can see the writing on the card: 5 something. He steps from the curb and crosses the roundabout.

The July sun beats against the steps of a nearby church where a man sits in a crumpled heap, his tears dripping on a bible spread open on his knees. The baker knows it would be right to stop and offer assistance. He continues on though, trusting that a priest will be along shortly to help the man.

At the entrance to the Métro a young man in an ill-fitting suit and flopping pocket square bounds up the stairwell, knocking the baker against a light post. The man carries an armful of flowers. He mumbles a hasty apology, checks his watch and ponders the street signs pointing in every direction. Finally he makes a decision, shoots his cuffs and sets off, his strides nervous, his trouser legs revealing knobby ankles with every stride.

After departing Beauvais, a December wind gathered itself and twisted into the fourth district of Paris. A boy stood shivering in a narrow passageway, his grandfather hunched beside him.

Concentrate, the old man said.

Henri Fournier was a month from his tenth birthday. His spectacles kept sliding down his nose as he stood on the open pages of a book.

Spread your arms, Henri.

The book had been bound in an animal skin dyed the colour of blood oranges, its edges long since darkened by the sweat of many hands. The case was embossed: a diamond shape, the four corners punched with pinholes. In the centre of the diamond, a pair of exotic slippers, toes curling upward, had been tooled into the leather. The design was faded, worn shallow with age, but could still be seen if one turned it at an angle to the light. Opened flat, the book was wide enough to carry Henri's feet, each to a page.

His grandfather believed the book magical, set in a font the old man had not seen in seventy years along the quays. Henri's father, proprietor of the family bookstall, wished the thing would be eaten by worms; for too long it had taken up space without returning a centime. Monsieur Fournier was quick to remind his son that no one trusted the invisible these days, and the less magic the better. Upon which Henri trusted his grandfather all the more.

Wider, Henri, palms up. Open your fingers.

The Fournier bookstall held too much poetry, mixed its philosophies with its mechanics and its travelogues among its fictions. It offered a selection of tattered orchestral scores, back issues of illustrated newspapers and postcards intended for the tourists: ten mademoiselles to a set. The stall was painted a peculiar shade of green, known to every bookseller on both banks of the river. They claimed the paint was a mysterious Fournier concoction, no doubt flammable, and depending on the season and time of day, it would glow. As though the stall were capable of producing its own light: lime green in the early morning, emerald at midday, mossy grey as the day faded.

If one stood on one's toes, one might snatch a glimpse over the stall and a view of the Pont des Arts.

Perfectly still now, my boy. Close your eyes.

Henri's face puckered; spots of light swam behind his eyelids. The old man whispered in his ear.

Do you feel anything?

I don't think so, Grandfather.

Your feet, Henri. Are they precise?

The boy squeezed his eyes behind his glasses. I can't see them.

Be certain, Henri. Without precision we are—?

Vague and lost, Grandfather.

Precisely. Quiet now. No scrunched faces.

The grandfather bent double, examining the position of Henri's feet. Left on the verso right on the recto, he muttered, and tapped at the toe of the boy's right boot. Henri crept his foot so as to not leave a scuff on the thick pages.

Careful, boy. And now?

Henri opened one eye. Nothing, Grandfather.

The old man moaned as he straightened up. Henri lowered his arms and released a cloud of breath. His mother, watching from the family apartment three floors up, called down to Henri.

Enough, young man. There are plenty of Fourniers in that godforsaken book trade already. No more games, the pair of you. Come in for supper before you freeze to death.

Off you go, the grandfather said. We will try again next summer.

The August downpour had settled to a fine drizzle. The Fournier men went off to scour the used bookshops near the university. Henri, halfway to his eleventh birthday and still in need of better spectacles, was left to mind the stall. Lingering puddles trickled off the lid.

Henri slapped at a drip on the back of his head, then moved his stool away from the stall. He worried about the heat, the sky beginning to cloud again, the books warping behind him, the postcards moulding, the itch in his bottom. He stood, sat again, squirmed, scratched, shook out his legs. He adjusted his spectacles, looked along the quay, upstream, downstream. There was no sign of his father and grandfather, nor the sound of their cart creaking under the weight of more volumes no one would buy. Henri began pacing from one end of the stall to the other, running a hand over the books, his fingers bouncing across the spines.

It was a game his grandfather had taught him, much to the dismay of his father, when Henri was hardly tall enough to reach the books. No peeking, the old man had said. Feel the books. When you think you are ready, make a selection.

Henri did as he was told, eventually pulling a slim volume from the rows in the stall, holding it against his forehead. The object of the game was to describe the case without seeing it.

The material, Henri. What do you feel? Fine linen or rough leather? Or both? And the stamping? The foil? You could try smelling it if you think it would help.

Can anyone actually smell a good book, Grandfather?

Of course not, the old man would bluster. All the buyer need do is hold it. As you are now. Let it rest in their hands. Curl fingers around the spine as if it were stitched for only them. Run a thumb along the soft edges of its pages. When they hold it, Henri, is when you have them. After that they can smell it all they like.

Henri chose a book and put it to his nose. A whiff of lavender. Henri pictured himself standing in a field of purple flowers. He turned at the sound of pounding hooves. A huge black horse sped past him at full gallop, the rider hunched in close to the mane, one arm brandishing a heavy sword. Henri saw the cruciform of a crusader sewn across the back of the rider's tunic. In the distance a castle smouldered with the fires of a siege.

Henri thought of purple.

He opened his eyes. The case was calfskin, as black as tar. The stamped design on the boards was ornate: tiny flowers in bloom, a twist of stems and leaves flowing across the case, over the spine and onto the back. The title had been foiled in copper, mottled now with the damp. Henri took another sniff. There was a faint odour of smoke.

His grandfather would have shaken his head. Purple, Henri? Wherever would you get such a notion?

Henri moved the stool closer to the stall and stretched his legs. He leaned against the green wood, pressed his spectacles against his nose, and opened the book.

Chapter One.

Henri's eyes kept snagging as the first paragraphs lazed their way to a beginning. A couple was strolling *gay and carefree* along a country riverbank. They approached from a distance, she in a *charmingly lovely* dress, the colour of *spring's own buttercups*; her hair *as rich and luminous as glittering chestnuts*. A wide-brimmed straw hat, *as graceful as the heavens*, shielded her *youthful and sun-kissed* face from the heat. Her companion was *crisply turned out* in morning suit, gloves, cravat, a pair of *immaculate spats*. His hand searched *romantically*, *longingly* to hold hers. And yet there were *morose and hateful* clouds in the sky, threatening *the freshest bloom of love*.

As he read *spring's own buttercups*, Henri cringed.

By page 20 the writer had finally gotten things moving. Henri could feel trouble rising from the typescript, the snags turning to jolts.

The lovers drew near, their voices grew louder. The woman *refused* her companion's gift. *You will forgive* me, the man *demanded in a blind rage*. The woman was *fearless*. She would not accept a book of poems from a *deceitful scoundrel* who kept her waiting. He protested, *fuming and lashing out*, *cursing her foolish schoolgirl pride*. No monsieur, she said in a *sharp and biting* voice, *you are the fool*. A thousand stanzas will *never pardon* a man who *betrays*. The *threatening* clouds turned *deadly black*, the woman in the yellow dress *pulled* her hand from his.

Betrays, thought Henri. Good word.

The skies above the couple released a torrent.

Henri looked up. His father was tossing books from the cart into the stall. His grandfather gathered lyric sheets in his arms. Within minutes the three Fourniers were drenched through. Henri's father threw up the front of the stall, dropped the lid and fumbled with the locks. The grandfather wiped his face with his sleeve and looked at the book in Henri's hands.

What happened to her?

To who? Henri said.

To *whom*, young man. The woman in the yellow dress.

I don't know. They were about to get caught in the rain.

His grandfather turned his grizzled face to the sky. Imagine that, he said.

The floods of 1910 would crest at the tops of the bookstalls. As the Seine retreated, a few hardy souls would return to tiptoe their way through the mud along the quays. They would find most of the green boxes closed: lids beginning to warp and strain at their locks, corners and seams oozing sludge, the rotting libraries within raising a gagging stench.

One stall appeared far from abandoned, its lid propped open. A pair of legs could be seen rising from its empty depths. Attached to the legs—thin ankles bare and pale in the cold air, splattered trousers bunching at the knees—a pair of feet in a young boy's boots, each dripping with black slime.

Head down in the stall, Henri shouted to his father. Dead, Papa!

Monsieur Fournier tipped his cap to a confused passerby and yelled back. Who's dead?

A cat, Papa! Drowned! Under Voltaire!

Which edition?

The fat one!

A mercifully instant death, then. Out you come. Bring the poor beast with you.

Henri wriggled free from the stall, his boots squishing on the quay. With the tail of the lifeless stray in one hand, he pushed his glasses against his nose with the other.

And so we get back to work, Monsieur Fournier said. The books return today.

They had left on the advice of the grandfather. The old man knew the river like a harbourmaster knew his shoals. A week before the water began rising, he asked if anyone could smell it. Smell what? Henri had said. Trouble, came the answer.

The books were packed, the postcards bundled, the newspapers baled with twine. Everything was piled on the family cart and the Fourniers, men and boy, pushed and pulled their way over the Pont des Arts. As they crossed they heard whirlpools foaming around the bridge's footings. Henri noticed his grandfather looking back across the river.

We saved them all, didn't we, Grandfather?

All but the unicorns, my boy.

Not every book would escape the flood. Those that at first glance had appeared like any other in the stall but on closer reading were different. Their magical plots and strange grammars had marked them, like a horn in the middle of an otherwise normal forehead. Different and misunderstood: thumbed briefly only to be put back, ignored altogether, and in the end left behind to be swallowed by the rising waters.

Unicorns? Henri said.

Your bible, Henri. Remember the story of Noah.

And the Ark?

Precisely. Which animal did not make the voyage?

You told me the unicorns had survived. They may be hard to see, you said, but they were still with us.

The grandfather smiled. That they are, Henri. And where would you find one, now that the river has carried them off?

Henri tapped a finger against his temple.

Precisely, the old man said.

The young woman hurries, her strides determined. Garlands of patriotic flags and bare light bulbs, limp and dismal in anticipation of the coming week's celebrations, stretch from building to building above her head. She realizes she is sweating.

Must you rush around, my dear? Have you forgotten what becomes of little girls who are not calm and careful?

She ignores her mother's voice, keeps her head down, breaks into a run; the scarf catches a puff of wind. She clutches at the fabric and returns it to cover her cheek.

Her other hand presses the parcel—a book of ancient tales, inscribed in a childlike hand—against her breast as though it were stolen treasure.

An infant, one always hoped, would bring change to any household. Certainly there would be more fatigue yet there would be more energy. There would be more laughter and more worry, one arriving hard after the other, and there would be warm naps under soft blankets and cold nights steaming away the croup. At the top of the cake-slice, life for the Notre-Dames did change, but hope had little to do with it.

As Octavio grew, his mother began to shrink. Madame picked at her meals, eating only a mouthful or two. Her dresses hung loose and wrinkled, her collars bent and crooked. She rarely slept, tossing and weeping quietly beside her husband. Dark circles appeared under her eyes. She had always carried herself with purpose; now she moved as if dazed, unsure of what to do or where to go next. Her smile, if one were to appear at all, was at best a thin stretch of lips. One minute she would plead with Monsieur to not open the bakery that day: the child was sure to fall out a window or be kidnapped by thieves or drown as she bathed him. The next she wouldn't hear Octavio's cries as he stumbled taking his first steps. There were days, however, when she found the will to work and brought the boy down to the shop. He would nestle in a basket or crawl around behind the counter. And it would be the customers who kept an eye on Octavio, fawning over every gurgle and coo, making sure no one stepped on his fingers if he ventured too close to the blue doors.

Sundays in the cake-slice had changed as well. Few could remember the last time they had seen Madame at mass. When Monsieur finished with his newspaper he would return upstairs and find his son under the kitchen table, banging wooden spoons or wobbling between the table's legs. Madame would be sitting there, turning a cold cup in her hand, absently moving a foot as the toddler Octavio careered past.

As though they were acrobats beginning their best

encore, Monsieur would tug Octavio out from under the table and onto his shoulders. We'll be out of your way, Monsieur would say to his wife, no trouble at all. Father and son would duck their heads as they climbed the circular stairs to the attic.

No trouble at all, Madame would say as she returned to staring out the window. Much as her husband had left her hours earlier, when he had gone to fetch his newspaper.

At ten minutes to eleven on the morning of the 21st of January, 1910, with a wondrous scientific precision, the gears and wheels of the city's public clocks stopped turning, their compressed-air power station flooded in the rising waters. Two days later the platforms of Gare d'Orsay were drowning in an oily pool ten metres deep, with unclaimed luggage bobbing through the water like rootless archipelagos.

Monsieur Notre-Dame leaned against the bakery doors. His newspaper offered readers a history of the floods that had inundated the city a month earlier.

Under the Pont des Arts the bloated river poured through the bridge's iron braces, the resulting whirlpools hissing, it was claimed by eyewitnesses, with the laughter of demons. By the 24th, seamstresses of the most elegant establishments along avenue Montaigne were being ferried to their sewing tables in skiffs poled by brave and noble watermen.

On the 29th the Seine began to fall.

Monsieur read none of it, content with his front page: today the Lady France, crowned in gold, cloaked in ermine, and wearing what the baker thought might be an expensive velvet gown. The woman towered over a flotilla of citizens, her outstretched arms inspiring them on as they rowed to the aid of flood victims trapped on the roofs of passing houses.

Swept up in the heroics, Monsieur did not notice a frown rising above his newspaper and creasing the face of Madame Lafrouche, concierge to an apartment house near the Boulangerie Notre-Dame.

The Lafrouches, husband and wife, had been devoted customers at the bakery since Monsieur was a teenager. Both were pleasant enough, though there seemed a touch of melancholy about the wife. When Madame Notre-Dame's pregnancy had grown too large to ignore, Madame Lafrouche had mysteriously stopped calling in for her daily order. In the months since, the woman had been seen trudging across the district to buy her breads from a bakery near the river. This excursion, she would bluster nervously to anyone that recognized her, was no less than cruelty, a strain on her swollen knees, and an insult to what had once been an unflagging loyalty to the Notre-Dames.

You are aware, monsieur, that the flooding has destroyed my bakery?

Monsieur looked up, then returned to the Lady France. How nice to see you again, Madame Lafrouche. It has been too long.

A bakery, I will remind you, that was clear across the district.

I am truly sorry, madame. My wife and I had no wish to offend.

Shameful it was, monsieur. To think that your marble produced the finest breads in the neighbourhood only to be reduced to a birthing table.

Indeed, madame, unforgivable. But I am afraid it was unavoidable.

Madame Lafrouche tapped her foot. I am now ready to return, she said.

Time heals all wounds, madame. You are most kind. I look forward to serving you tomorrow morning.

Kindness has nothing to do with it, monsieur. I return only because of my Alphonse. The man is beyond hope.

Monsieur repeated that he was sorry. Madame Lafrouche raised an eyebrow.

As you should be, monsieur. After all it is your sourdough that infects my husband's brain. Where else will I find such a loaf, he moans. Return to Notre-Dame's, he cries. I implore you, he pleads. Why, were it up to me Alphonse would be fetching his own bread or going hungry. But I am not one to shirk my wifely duties.

You are an honour to the profession, madame.

Madame Lafrouche pulled a package wrapped with purple iridescent paper from her handbag. Her voice quivered and caught in her throat.

I wish I were, monsieur. Nonetheless, I hear you have a fine son.

Monsieur's ink-stained fingers smudged the shining paper as he opened the gift: a book, bound in green linen, its endpapers a garden of floral purples and yellows. The end of a red satin ribbon peeked from between the pages. Wiping his hands on his trousers, Monsieur fanned through the book, stopping here and there at an illustration.

Madame Lafrouche rearranged the contents of her handbag. The *Arabian Nights*, she said. Alphonse's idea, of course.

Monsieur studied the illustrations. In one an old

fisherman dressed in rags clutched at a basket spouting a whirlwind of strange smoke; in another a black-skinned giant, one eye glowing in the middle of his forehead, wiped his greasy lips as he crouched on a pile of human bones.

All very fantastical, I am sure, Madame Lafrouche said. Hardly readable at all. Still, it did come from Printemps.

As you say, madame. Hardly readable at all.

Monsieur retreated into the bakery. He returned with a golden loaf, its dome scored with the initials N-D.

Yesterday's best batch, madame. With my compliments to your husband.

The woman tucked the loaf under her arm and spun on her heel, leaving Monsieur to admire a fellow like Alphonse Lafrouche, still doting on a wife who had lost two pregnancies to fevers and miscarriage. A fellow who without a second thought would send his darling Geneviève shopping along the boulevards. All on a taximan's wages.

Sitting in the attic window with his son nestled in his lap, Monsieur Notre-Dame would slowly turn the pages of the *Arabian Nights*. When he reached an illustration, Octavio would laugh and point.

A beginning then, Monsieur would say.

He told the boy his stories. They were conjured out of his head, tales that had little to do with the pictures in the book, the flying horses or the thieves in their treasure caves or the scruffy boy with his magic lamp. Monsieur told them not as the book might have, but as *he* saw them, jumping to life before his own eyes.

Leaving Madame tossing under the duvet and his son murmuring in the armoire drawer, Monsieur Notre-Dame slipped out of bed.

From the back of a kitchen cupboard his wife had never been able to reach, Monsieur retrieved Octavio's book. He opened it to the back and found a spot in the bottom corner of the endpaper. He scrounged a nub of pencil, sat at the kitchen table, and waited for his writing hand to stop trembling.

F F F From teh the liba library fo of Oct a v oi io ND.
Boula ger ieNoterNotreDame. 8th. Parsi Par ppp Paris.

The baker turns a last corner and finds the pavement blocked by a rag woman pushing a cart piled high with clothes. She wears a leaning tower of three hats, each progressively smaller than the one beneath.

As he steps aside to let the woman pass, something unfamiliar flares the baker's nostrils.

His legs ache as he runs for home. The smell of smoke closes in with every breathless stride.

Months after the Seine had burst it banks, sodden rubble and drowned rats were still being swept from the streets. The stench of manure sluiced from upriver farms had slowly faded to a telltale sniff. Shoppers had returned to the boulevards, a new season appeared in the shop windows, life was once again anticipation.

Pascal Normande stood in the doorway of his shop working his watch chain like a string of prayer beads. He checked the time, squinted into the sky. Events, surely, must have progressed by now. He could barely contain himself. The madness of being master of his

domain yet completely at the mercy of a woman's natural ways made his head pound.

He kept up appearances by pacing the fabric tables
and snapping at assistants, mopping at his brow and
spying out from between the legs of the mannequins in
his windows. He regretted promising a sou to the messenger, who—if the boy knew what was good for him—
would arrive in the next ten seconds with news that
Monsieur was at last a father and Madame would soon
return to the business of the shop. Very well, he thought.
Perhaps a franc, should the news grant his secret wish.

But the new season invaded these giddy thoughts.
It was not a good time to be birthing babies. A Normande
client expected timeliness, not time away. The new collection was weeks from being finished; the flood had
caused infuriating delays.

From behind a skirt, Pascal took another look outside,
then shut his watch. He turned to a passing seamstress.

One more minute or the boy gets nothing, he said.

A small dog waddled around the mannequins'
ankles and under Pascal's nose. The animal panted in
the heat of the window, not knowing it would become
a gift for a newborn child, in time a gift named Zouzou.
All the dog knew at this moment was its need for
relief. It raised a hind leg and pissed into a shoe the
colour of ripe strawberries.

Beast! My best Louis heels! Ruined!

Pascal took a breath, steadied his nerves, and gently lifted the pup from the spreading puddle, the messenger ran into the shop. Pulling off his cap, the boy thrust out an expectant palm. The smile on Pascal's face stretched broad and toothy.

Well?

Congratulations, monsieur. You have your girl.

And Madame?

Everyone is fine, monsieur.

Pascal looked at the messenger's still-extended hand. He handed the dog to the boy and dug into his waist-coat pocket.

Would ten do?

The customers of Atelier Normande were divided. Some maintained that despite the ballooning waist, the swollen feet, the rashes and moods, and the incessant perspiration that ruined one dress after another, Madame Céleste was transformed into an adoring parent because she at last possessed an accessory of her own design.

She will have her mother's eyes, someone said. The deepest brown or I don't know my business.

A nose sure to be aquiline, said another, and a mouth that will be the loveliest of budding roses.

The little one's hair, friends. Like pure cocoa: not so thin as to hang limp but not so thick as to be unruly.

Nature shall see to it. The child will grow to perfection, a sight to behold.

Others were less superficial. For them it was merely nature taking its proper course. No couple, not even one as matched as Céleste and Pascal, was truly whole without children.

Nature has already seen to it.

Madame has been transformed because now she is the complete woman.

A prouder father you will never find.

The child will be a Normande through and through.

And all the better for it.

Pascal thought the name Isabelle was suitable. After my mother, he said.

Nine months had given Madame time to consider other possibilities. An early favourite had been Eugénie, for the tall and elegant wife of Napoleon III, but Madame quickly realized that the resulting nickname—Nenya—would never do. There were the famous actresses of the cabarets: Yvettes and Gabrielles and a singer named Polaire whose picture appeared in the papers almost weekly. The possibility that she might give birth to a boy had never entered Madame's mind.

No, she said. The name needs to be something distinctive. Feminine. With a note of strength.

Like her mother, Pascal said.

Isabeau Normande's eyes did indeed become the deepest brown, yet her nose showed a slightly crooked angle. Her mouth did not bloom so much as wander a bit wide and a bit askew. And her hair served as a rich match to her eyes, chocolate to be sure, but invariably in a disappointing tangle.

The seamstresses of Atelier Normande set to work creating miniature versions of Madame Céleste's wardrobe. Soon enough mother and daughter began their shopping excursions. In the Galeries Lafayette they wandered hand in hand among the mannequins, Isabeau learning to judge quality by removing a glove and running a finger along a seam. In Printemps they sat at the newly created cosmetics counter, Madame guiding Isabeau's nervous hand as it smudged rouge all over her cheeks. In Samaritaine they took lunch in the rooftop restaurant, the maître d' suggesting a table overlooking the river.

Madame nodded with pride as the waiter pulled out Isabeau's chair, as the girl smoothed her dress once she had climbed up and settled herself, as she did her best to fold a napkin across her lap and asked politely for a glass of milk.

On a window seat in her parents' apartments Isabeau Normande pulled at her stockings. A pleasant four-year-old by now, bored with watching a summer Sunday pass along the street.

She climbed from the window and bounced to the doors leading to her parents' study. Balancing on one foot, Isabeau slid the doors apart, the other keeping her dog at bay. Her father shifted in his chair, his snoring interrupted. We are working, child, he said.

Pascal Normande fell back to dozing. His shoes were off, his belly popping through an unbuttoned waistcoat. Madame Céleste was perched on a settee. The newspaper in her hands shouted of political troubles in the Balkans. ANARCHY IN THE STREETS! ASSASSINATION! WAR IS CERTAIN! Without looking up from the paper, she suggested Isabeau run along to see why Cook insisted on lighting the stove when the apartment was already stifling enough and wouldn't a chilled soup be easier on everyone.

Cook stood at a table slicing carrots, a large pot simmering behind her. Isabeau made a face at the mound of vegetables awaiting the chop. The woman mopped her forehead and waved the girl and her dog from the kitchen.

In the lounge Isabeau flopped on a chaise, her feet dangling off the edge. She stared at the ceiling, attempted to wiggle her ears, picked at her nose. She rose from the chaise and skated around the room, her stockings sliding on the gleaming wood.

She pulled a fashion magazine from an arranged display on a side table. Lying on the floor, knocking her heels behind her, she pushed the dog away and propped herself on her elbows. She flipped through the pages to an illustration of a young woman, her head veiled in a cascade of lace falling from the brim of her hat. The dog padded across the magazine and licked at Isabeau's nose. Isabeau pushed the dog off the magazine.

Zouzou! You mustn't walk on Maman's women!

The animal persisted, nipping at her sleeve, tearing a seam and leaving a flap of fabric hanging loose.

Isabeau jumped to her feet. Beast! Now look what you've done. Maman will be very angry!

The dog crouched in anticipation. Isabeau darted around the chaise, made for the door, pretended a turn for the study, slid to a stop. The dog's head followed her every move around the room. Isabeau ran from the lounge and headed for the kitchen.

Through the swinging door, Isabeau skipped around

the table, waving her arms above her head. The dog tried to follow, legs churning, claws clicking on the tiles. Cook scraped a mound of celery into her boiling pot and returned to the cutting board. The pot handle hovered over the edge of the stove, a snag waiting for a torn sleeve.

The dog cocked its head at the shrill noise suddenly coming from its playmate. Isabeau stood frozen, her fingers as locked as talons, reaching to tear at her face. Cook dropped the knife, shouting to be heard over the girl's howls.

The spilt water went cool in an instant on the floor. Curls of onion lay scattered under the table. Zouzou lapped at the puddle as Isabeau was led screaming from the kitchen.

The scald became a scar, an embossed stroke melting down the forehead, looping around an eye still the richest brown, forming an irregular pool on the cheek, dribbling away at the line of the jaw. As though an artist both gifted and unkind had set to work, dabbing varnish on what might best catch the light, beginning a delicate line of white where the scar met the hairline, weaving that thin stroke through long, dark strands.

The scar in turn became a reflex, turning young Isabeau's head down and away, allowing locks of hair to fall over the marred side of her face. She learned how to train the errant strands behind her ear, leaving enough slack in the length to distract curious eyes.

On sunnier days she might be found in the apartment's entry hall, a corridor of mirrors, each in a grand frame, their bevelled edges throwing a rainbow around whatever passed in their reflections. When the low light of afternoon bounced through the hall, Isabeau would select a picture from one of her mother's magazines.

The model's head would fill the page, turning to the viewer with a demure lift to her chin and a graceful arc of the neck. Isabeau would fold the page length-wise, then stand in front of the mirrors. She would bring the magazine to her face, sliding the folded page until the bridge of the model's nose met the bridge of her own. A new face looked back, reflected in the mirrors on the opposite wall, repeating itself into a chorus of half-smiles.

The fire brigade arrives. A dozen men merge into a single mass of action. They prepare in silence, absorbed in their work, as the captain repeats his Stand Aside Madames, Mind Yourself Little Ones, Make Way Monsieurs. Faced with such resolve, the crowd in front of the cake-slice jostles to clear a path to the bakery's front step.

To reach the fire on the top floors, the brigade pries open the blue doors and rushes through the shop. They take no notice of the empty display case, the wicker baskets awaiting another day's assortments, the vignettes painted on the walls' yellowing tiles. Heavy boots leave black streaks on the polished marble floors.

Following his men, the captain is momentarily distracted. A portrait sketched in pencil—a young woman—hangs in a simple frame above the door to the cellar. Half the portrait is obscured. A thick curve of hair, streaked with a wisp of white, casts a shadow across the face. Only the subject's visible eye, glistening and dark, with its brow arched, looks back at him.

Reminding his men to keep their fool heads on their shoulders and their eyes out front, the captain lingers as the brigade stampedes past him. He watches them disappear to the rear of the building, then pulls off his heavy gloves. Kissing the tips of his fingers, he touches them to the portrait.

Wish us luck, mademoiselle.

The brigade climbs the stairwell to the top landing, wrestling hose and axe and each other into what remains of the baker's apartment. By now roofless and gutted to black wooden bones, venting smoke into the July air and snowing books on the crowd below.

The masters suggested he try working in the open air. A decidedly rougher approach, they said, and certainly not how we did things in our day, but a windy afternoon on the quayside or an evening in the parks picking insects off one's canvas might focus Monsieur Kalb's rather vague abilities.

Fog hung over the Pont des Arts. Jacob removed a bundle of sticks from his tattered carpetbag. He loosened the leather straps around the bundle, the masters droning in his ears.

Have it in your mind's eye, Monsieur Kalb.

Jacob hitched his sagging trousers, opened a few hinges and spread the stick ends. He ignored the stiffness in his joints, the grime under his long fingernails, the evening's chill. Finally he stood a rickety easel by the railing.

See the truth, Monsieur Kalb.

Jacob pulled a small canvas from the bag—

Art is truth, Monsieur Kalb.

—then placed it on the easel's shelf.

Square and level, Monsieur Kalb. If your work is to be more than scribble.

Jacob stepped back from the easel, his eyes following the river as it slid into the mist. Buildings, soft blocks of blue-grey, merged with the sky. In the flat light, trees along the quayside became swaths of a darker grey. Staring at the blank canvas, Jacob struggled to summon a finished landscape.

See it, Monsieur Kalb. As though it were finished and put aside to dry.

So here I find my Señor Kalb, hard at work.

Jacob spun around. The one they called el Bárbaro, a classmate from the Academy, stood looking at Jacob's blank canvas.

And so I am sad for it. My Kalb has found no truth today.

Jacob felt his throat tighten, his hands go clammy. The urge to reach out and touch his friend shuddered through him. The Barbarian smiled.

You are too anxious, mi amigo. That is why tonight we will ignore your worries. We will eat like the monkeys we are, drink to our organ grinders and curse them from the other side of our greasy mouths. They tell us that art is truth as we dance at the end of our leashes. So we will howl that it is life that is true and they will stop cranking their little music boxes and we will do some living. Agreed?

Jacob turned out his pockets.

The weather was miserable today, he said. The gardens were deserted, no one was sitting. I sold nothing.

The Barbarian pulled his mouth into a clown's pout, his eyes smiling.

But then I am not sad, mi amigo. I hear rumours of a tableau this evening. Free of charge, drinks on the house. Everyone will be there.

There had been other evenings: a week earlier, a month or more perhaps, or in those first days of the Academy. For all Jacob could remember, they may as well have been dreams.

A sticky floor spinning under his feet. Deafening shouts and manic laughter fill his ears. Out of nothing a painting rushes at him. Manet's *Déjeuner sur l'herbe*: its every detail as sharp as broken glass. Slices of picnic and bodies float before his eyes. In the foreground, the artist's pale-skinned nude shifts her pose, her wide black eyes looking directly at Jacob.

Do you enjoy what you see, monsieur?

In the corner of a cellar bar, Jacob's arm snakes around someone's waist. They are weaving drunk, taking turns imitating their teachers. The reek of stale bodies and spilt beer makes the air almost solid. A make-shift stage stands empty in the centre of the room. Behind the bar a poster: ANOTHER LUNCHEON! ONE SITTING ONLY!

Two young men solemnly step on stage. Dressed in ragged suits, they arrange themselves in front of a stained bedsheet hung from the rafters, the impression of a forest glade painted across it. Scrounged baskets appear, their contents—rotten fruit, spent corks, stale ends of bread—are scattered around the two men. The audience, crushed into the dim room, whistles and stamps their feet and bellows for more.

A boy, no more than fifteen, shuffles into the scene. He wears a threadbare curtain for a toga. Blinking in the haze of cigarette smoke, the boy poses as if picking a flower from the glade. As he bends forward he fumbles to keep his costume from falling open.

An older man, dimpled plump and naked, jumps into the scene. Covered in white powder, he tiptoes to the centre of the group. He curtsies and takes his place, reclining in front of his picnic companions. He places one elbow on an upturned knee, rests his chin in his hand and turns to the crowd. He becomes Manet's nude, if only for an instant, his lips slick with rouge and widening into a theatrical smile.

Do you enjoy what you see, my friends?

The cellar explodes in applause.

Jacob stumbles from an alleyway, pulling up his trousers. It is minutes or hours later. The sound of the Barbarian calling his name echoes off the walls behind him.

Jacob was asked to leave the Academy later that term, the masters explaining that, while your portraiture shows promise, Monsieur Kalb, your landscapes lack even a basic vision. They said his prospects for improvement appeared equally dim. He was wished well in finding another occupation, perhaps drawing posters for the theatre marquees or cartoons for the newspapers. In these pursuits the masters expressed confidence that he could apply their lessons regarding the art of the face. It is the eyes, they reminded him, where all would be revealed.

Jacob said nothing throughout the meeting. None of the masters looked directly at him.

On the landing outside the attic room of a traveller's hotel, the manager's wife stood with her hands buried in the pouch of her apron, silently cursing her husband for not having the backbone to deliver eviction notices himself.

She watched Jacob Kalb pack his tools: a paintbox, three brushes, a few pencils, one stick of charcoal, a dulled penknife, the folding easel, a small square of rolled canvas, his sketching book.

It is a black day, monsieur. But the rent, you see. You and I are months behind.

I wish my skills had paid better, Jacob said.

The manager's wife looked into the room. Tacked to the ceiling was a jumbled gallery of small landscapes, half-finished watercolours, oil sketches, drawings in ink and pencil. All lights and tones and weathers, every manner of sky, the same view along the Seine. In each a few birds hovered above the river, and barely visible, the same silhouetted figures walked beneath the trees.

Where will you go? the woman said.

Under the stars for a while, I think.

The manager's wife poked Jacob in the ribs.

You are too thin for the bohemian life, monsieur.

Sell a few pictures. For once carry some coins in your pocket. Pay some rent.

He lived near the food markets for a time. He wanted to paint the noisy chicken men, the overflowing mounds of vegetables, the fat and happy fishwives, the porters with their enormous mushroom hats. But when the smell of rotting cabbages and yesterday's cheese seeped into one hovel after another, Jacob moved on. It was the scalded piglets, their eyelashes caught in mid-flutter, their tails still curled in death, that forced him from the markets for good. He found a dry corner tucked high under the arches of the Pont des Arts, staking his claim with all he owned.

All contained in his carpetbag. The paint supplies, the remains of a woollen sweater, a pair of fingerless gloves, mismatched socks, the thick corduroy jacket he had worn on his first day in Paris, a tin of scrounged cigarette ends. Only his sketching book, refreshed with the money he made touting portraits, was stiff with blank pages. A square of canvas, rolled so it might not crease, nestled between the bag's handles.

On this one canvas Jacob would make a fresh attempt each day. And if the sun clouded over or the winds picked up, he would unclamp the day's work from his easel and make his way to the river's edge. Laying it on the surface of the water, he would slide the canvas back and forth in the current. As tendrils of colour wafted downstream, the numb in his fingers would creep to his wrists. The tints of green he had used to render the bookstalls were the last to dissolve.

At night he would lay the blank canvas beside him as he slept. If the river mist lay low, it might be dry by first light. Dry enough for another day and another start on the bridge.

For Jacob the booksellers along the quays became a variety troupe of live models. Some went bare-headed; some wore hats. Some pushed spectacles to their foreheads; others slumped and snored. There were thick scarves around scrawny necks, too-small overcoats over too-wide shoulders, old boots and rope shoes. Each guarded his stall with everything from walking sticks and dusters to well-aimed tobacco spits and loud curses. Each had peculiar rituals of opening for the day or closing up for the night. They may have squirmed on the same stools or smoked under the same trees or wished with one mind that the occasional passerby would just move along and stop disturbing them, yet each was as different as the books they offered.

Not long after moving to the river, Jacob noticed a particular bookstall. It was the colour that caught his eye: how the green changed the higher or lower the sun, the duller or brighter the sky. He tried including the stall in his landscapes, spent weeks adjusting his mixes: Prussian blue and Indian yellow for the evening shades of deep green; thalo blue, cadmium yellow, a drop of alizarin crimson for its morning sage; its midday lime green requiring a generous brushful of lemon yellow.

The stall appeared to have three proprietors. One was old and bent, the second flabby and middle-aged, the third a young man, perhaps in his teen years. Jacob assumed it was a family-run concern; the young one had drawn the short straw. He occupied the stool most every day.

In the evenings, as the sun dipped behind the buildings along the quay, Jacob would watch as the young bookseller removed a large volume from the stall. The boy would peer up and down the quay, satisfy himself that no one was approaching, and place the book on the pavement. Sliding his spectacles to the top of his head, the bookseller would plant his feet on the book's open pages, lift his arms out from his sides and turn his face to the sky.

The baker drops his books, searches frantically for a path through the crowd. As they move aside some turn away, ashamed they could do nothing, unable now to watch a man they have known all his life meet such a tragedy. A few call out that they are with him.

Remember who you are, monsieur. Remember your father. Be a Notre-Dame.

The old fellow with the thick spectacles steps into the baker's path.

I am sorry, my friend. They are all gone now.

The elderly woman who had been shouting

directions reaches from the edge of the crowd.

My dearest boy, thank the Lord you are safe.

The baker sees no one, hears no comfort.

He shrugs the old man's hand off his shoulder and reaches the blue doors. He cannot remember leaving them open. Running past the counter and the empty baskets, he follows a trail of boot prints to the rear stairwell and takes the steps two at a time.

Octavio Notre-Dame was as thin as his father, though his hands were strong and nimble for one so young. His mother had given him a head of black hair that behaved only when oiled and pushed under a hat. Yet the boy's eyes were his own; as small as collar buttons, the brightest grey, one crowned with a brow that arched slightly higher than the other. As though he were about to share a secret.

In a stifling room of six-year-olds, each scratch and twitch pushing faith in the innocence of boys to its edge, a Sister of Grace chalked numbers on a black-board: 1349; 1431; 1572; 100,000; 1793; 16.

The nun turned to face her students. Gentlemen, she said, we will now review our histories.

Octavio sank his chin deep into his collar; his fingers clenched under the desk. He whispered to himself.

Monsieur Notre-Dame? the Sister said. She drew a line under 1349.

Fingernails digging into his hands, Octavio mut-tered the word *plague*.

LOUDER, MONSIEUR. That God might hear you.

1349, Sister. The Black Death.

Continue, the woman said. She stamped at each number with her chalk.

1431, Sister. Joan of Arc burned alive.

1572. Saint Bartholomew's Day. 100,000 killed by the Catholics.

1793. King Louis guillotined.

Which Louis would that be, monsieur?

16, Sister.

Very good. And the 100,000?

Octavio watched the nun's wrinkled face melt into that of Saint Joan. The girl's pale skin crackled in the fire while her dripping armour formed a pool at the front of the class. She kept asking Octavio why. Why so many had to perish.

Notre-Dame? the Sister said.

Octavio wished they had not shaved poor Joan's head.

NOTRE DAME!

The maid of Orléans vanished in a burst of flame.

Because they were Protestants, Sister.

It is the boy's shoes, madame.

The school's curé had summoned Madame Notre-Dame. Sitting in the young priest's office, her eyes wandered over a map of the holy lands pinned to the wall behind him.

Madame?

Shoes, Father. You were saying.

On the wrong feet, I'm afraid. It is a sign.

Madame felt the cool of Gabriel's whisper on the nape of her neck.

Let this be a lesson, Immacolata.

Madame flicked a hand at her ear as though brushing away a bothersome fly.

A message, Father?

You could say, madame. Or a symptom.

His shoes. On the wrong feet.

Constantly, said the curé.

It is hard enough to remind him to wear shoes at all.

Madame, this is not about being forgetful. It is about Octavio's word-blindness.

Blindness, Father? My boy sees well enough.

True, but what he does not see is his left from right. Somewhere between his eyes and his feet the signal goes astray. His brain does not connect the two. He sees his feet and he sees his shoes but he does not see them fitting together.

Madame turned her head sideways, following the Jordan as it disappeared into the Dead Sea. The curé continued.

The boy knows his letters. He knows the words they should make but cannot put them in order. His brain mixes them up, or turns them backwards or upside down. Sometimes he loses them altogether. Trust me, madame, I have made inquiries, read the studies, consulted the latest theories. The experts call it the word-blindness. It is something quite new in the field.

Madame creased her brow. You are saying he does not read like the other boys?

Cannot read, madame, cannot. Not much more than his own name. I am afraid his letters are also beyond hope.

Madame Notre-Dame felt her eyes welling again. The crying came on almost daily now.

You will not feel as mothers feel.

The curé handed her a sheet of paper splattered with ink, tiny fingerprints, a scrawled mess of handwriting.

The students have been studying their Genesis, madame. Your son wrote this.

in hte degining
In the beginning dog
In the beginning god God crates the hevens the heavens
and the eart earth in the beginning God
in the degining
in In the beginning God created the hevens heavens and the
earth. the the The earth was wtout without form anb void,
and the bark bar darkness was uq upon upon the face of the
deeq pppp Beginning Beginning Beginning

His father's son, Madame Notre-Dame said. She handed the paper to the priest.

And a good and pleasant boy, madame. Small for his age, keeps to himself, but clever in his own way. He does very well with his sums. Shows a true gift for numbers and dates. He constantly amazes the Sisters with his memory. Historical events, battles, conquests, the reigns of kings and queens, that sort of thing. It is all most remarkable, considering.

Considering, Father?

He will never learn like other children. The boy falls further behind every day. Numbers and rote have their place but they cannot stretch a brain so disconnected. Art, literature, philosophy—none of these will be Octavio's. He will never lead what they call a life of the mind.

Madame's eyes spilled over.

My dear woman, the curé said, there is no need for tears. Keep your faith in the Lord. Like all our sins, the boy's weakness is simply part of a greater plan.

Madame groped at her sleeves for a handkerchief. Father, when I met my husband I was content with what heaven had in store. My Emile's stories were charming; they made me laugh, they made me fall in love. I did not care that he could not read. In fact I loved him all the more. He was not ashamed of—what did you call it—his weakness. How then could I be? He said the Notre-Dames were always too busy working to be reading books. So God gave me my proud Emile and I accepted him as he was. With all my heart. Is that not faithful enough?

One does not bargain with one's duty to God, madame.

All I wanted in return, Father, was that the Lord bless me—bless Emile and I—with a child. It seemed so little to ask. To be given as you give. Are children not a gift from God? I knew the risks and I told Gabriel as much. I knew a child might inherit his father's fate, as Emile had inherited his. And I have tried with every waking moment since to be a good mother. But now for my selfishness my boy is to be punished. To have no mother at all and now to be sent away. You must not do this, Father. None of this is his sin, it is mine.

Madame, I am certain you are a fine mother and that you only want what is best for your son. Then trust us to do this for him. Octavio will do better to stay at home. When he comes of age he will take up your husband's trade and no doubt do it proud. Be assured that Gabriel has heard you. He knows what you have done. It is up to us to see His plan through. We need only give Octavio a situation with, shall we say, less intellect. The boy will thrive; I promise you. And the Lord will be pleased.

A lesson, Immacolata, to the selfish.

Walking home, Madame thought about the marble table in the cellar of the bakery. Emile's worried face, the last searing contraction, the sound of her child's first murmur. Then the darkness closing in as she tried to claw out of a hole only to slide deeper. The wet earth under her fingernails.

She felt her knees giving out, she worried she would collapse on the pavement. She saw herself lying by the curb, pedestrians huddled over her. Madame gripped her son's hand, praying for that tiny pink fist she had seen rising from the bowl to hold her up. She wondered if Gabriel was even listening, if he had ever heard a word.

Octavio dared not complain that his mother's grip was hurting him or that he couldn't keep up or that he might drop his satchel or that she was frightening him. As they approached the cake-slice, she suddenly let go of his hand and stopped in the middle of the street, her shoulders heaving. Octavio stammered that he was sorry—everything was going to be all right—the other boys weren't going to tease him anymore—she wouldn't have to walk him to school—please stop crying—I promise promise promise to be good.

He ran through the doors of the bakery to find his father.

Reaching the top landing, the baker stops at the sight of his front door off its hinges, cracked and warped, scarred by axe handles, paint bubbled in the heat. The brigade captain comes out of the apartment and moves the door to one side. The baker tries to push past, managing a glimpse over the man's broad shoulder: square towers that had once formed walls of colour, standing now as melted grey bricks silhouetted against open sky. The captain keeps a grip on the baker.

There's nothing to be done, monsieur.

I hear I am to have a new apprentice, Monsieur said.

Emile Notre-Dame did not stop dividing a mound of dough as his wife told him of her visit to the school. He calmly put aside one of the halves, floured the table and reached for his rolling pin. As Madame left the cellar he began flattening out the dough. Then, for the second time in his life, he spoke with God.

He asked the Lord where His cruelty had come from.

You punish another innocent boy, the next Notre-Dame to come along, for the stupidity of his father. What have any of us done to deserve this curse?

He wanted to know how God dared to break a good woman's heart.

She had wanted so much to be a mother, if only you could have let her be one.

He reminded God about their first conversation. How he had thanked every angel and saint as he kneeled at the wedding altar for escorting his Immacolata all the way from Tuscany, through the sharks and mermaids, to kneel beside a humble fellow from the eighth.

And now you condemn her to this cellar.

Monsieur's rolling pin split end to end as he swung it against the marble.

The air was heavy that evening in the Notre-Dame apartment. Her supper plate untouched, Madame had left the kitchen table and closed the bedroom door behind her. Monsieur watched his wife disappear, then slid his chair next to Octavio's. They stared at their hands. The baker finally spoke.

I wasn't much for school either. We Notre-Dames have always found other ways to entertain ourselves.

Minutes passed in silence. Sixteen fingers were crossed, four thumbs slowly turned. As Octavio began to squirm in his chair, a pigeon landed outside on the kitchen's windowsill.

Have I told you the one about the birds? Monsieur said.

Octavio shook his head. Monsieur unlinked his hands and laid them flat on the table.

Very well. Imagine a time before this.

When there lived an emperor like no other. He hosted no feasts and wrote no laws. Foreign kings never visited him; ambassadors did not drop in to ask for treaties; he sent no armies to invade his neighbours. He did not live in a palace, was never entertained by travelling minstrels, he declared no holidays. He was not a tyrant locking enemies away in his dungeons, nor was he a madman commanding the sun to reduce its heat. This emperor was a simple man, like his father before him, and his father's father, and his father's father's father before that. A good and simple man.

But still an emperor, Octavio said.

Like no other, Monsieur said. But one with a secret.

Monsieur watched his son's eyes grow wide, then lowered his voice. The emperor, he whispered, was not wise enough to be an emperor at all.

Or so he thought. As a boy the emperor felt out of place. The children around him seemed to be smarter than he. Whenever he asked how they came to know so much, they would smile and shrug their shoulders. A little bird told us, they would laugh. Growing to manhood, his awkwardness remained. As much as the emperor tried to learn, as much as he tried to understand, as much as he thought he knew, others acted as though they knew more.

As the emperor's domain was a city of grand buildings and fine leafy trees, so it was a haven for birds. The citizens of the city loved their feathered companions, offered them every perch and comfort, delighted in every song they sang.

But still the birds did not speak to the emperor? Octavio said.

Patience, my boy. As much as everyone loved the birds, some citizens loved the sound of their own voices. Idle talk flew through the streets like the birds themselves. With all this gossip the emperor knew his secret would be discovered. He would be laughed at and called a fool.

The emperor needed to find a way to hide his secret. So one day he dressed in the finest clothes he owned. He polished his shoes and combed his hair and scrubbed his face. Then he called on the city's greatest artist. I would like my portrait done, he said. Paint me as you see me. Do not make me taller or thinner or handsomer. I want only a true likeness, plain and simple.

But was he handsome? Octavio said.

The ladies would swoon wherever he walked, Monsieur said. Now where was I?

The painting, Papa.

Right. The artist was finished within the month, and the emperor was very pleased. Looking at his portrait was like looking in a mirror. He squinted his eyes, tilted his head, examined the details from this side and that. He began wondering about the man in front of him. What would this fellow look like with different clothes? Who would he be if he wore a beard? Or a hat? At last it came to him.

Octavio sat up straight.

The emperor imagined himself as someone else, Monsieur said.

Octavio wrinkled his brow. Monsieur carried on.

In his mind the emperor stopped slouching, he drew back his shoulders. His nose straightened, a confident smile appeared. He became a man who could walk the streets with his head held high, his face glowing in the sun. Here was a man that the birds of the city would not only speak to, but would also be perfectly happy to come and live with. Here was the portrait of a wise man.

So, as someone else, the emperor went out to gather a few birds.

At first he did not know which ones he should bring home. He knew nothing of their names or their origins or their habits. He only admired their variety, their plumage, the ones he could hold in his hand. He pictured how they might look collected in his rooms. And that was how he chose them, one by one.

For years the emperor assembled his birds. They took up every nook and corner. Their cages became his furniture: propping his windows open, levelling his crooked bed, acting as tables and chairs and shelves to hold even more cages. Some birds were no bigger than the eggs that had hatched them; with feathers so bright they hurt his eyes. Some were huge beasts, ugly and brown and dull. A few would not stop chattering, annoying and loud. There were scrawny birds and plump birds and clever birds and silly birds and birds that made no sound at all.

Did they ever speak to the emperor, Papa?

Not so fast, Monsieur answered.

The city watched the emperor's collection grow larger and more unwieldy. While they could see the emperor was wise, for who could not be with so many birds under his roof, they also knew his birds would grow restless, as birds eventually do. In time he would have to release them. But still the emperor brought home more and more birds. Finally his rooms could hold no more. And that was when it happened.

Monsieur's voice trailed off, an effect he had learned from his father.

What happened? Octavio said.

The birds disappeared, Monsieur said. One day while the emperor was out, the birds released themselves. He returned home to find his rooms empty, every cage open, every perch vacant. No one had heard them leave. No one saw the sky darken with a cloud of wings.

The emperor mourned the loss of his birds. Being surrounded by them had been his greatest pleasure and now that joy was gone. But worse still he knew that he would never be seen as wise. The citizens would learn that his birds had left and would begin their nosy questions: how could a man with so many birds not know how to keep them? The emperor would have no answers and they would march him out of the city.

Did they march him away? Octavio asked.

Not quite, Monsieur said. You see, the more the emperor worried about the birds he had lost, the more he could see them in his mind's eye. As clearly as if they were still crowding his rooms. Then he remembered his own portrait. How he had imagined the man standing before him. Could he do such a thing with his memories of his birds? Like the one that had lived above his kitchen cupboard, a smelly, moulting thing it was. Could he see that little fellow suddenly bouncing up and down like a bird twice its size, puffing its green chest feathers and crooning to the females at the other end of the shelf? Or the bird with the giant yellow bill that had spent every day perched on the back of the emperor's armchair, picking at loose threads and making a mess of things. Could he imagine it raising its grand beak, coughing once or twice, then reciting a poem?

Could he, Papa?

He could and he did, Monsieur said. The emperor discovered there was no little bird telling anybody anything. Indeed it wasn't birds he had needed at all. The pictures in his head would make him wise.

A good and simple emperor, Octavio said.

Monsieur stopped pacing around the kitchen table. That is why we Notre-Dame men need our pictures, he said.

Like your newspapers, Papa?

The thinnest baker in all Paris smiled. We shall look at them together. This Sunday we make a start.

The brigade captain has seen it all before. Too many versions of *I was only gone for a moment*. Someone steps out to retrieve his mail, leaves a candle too close to a wafting curtain, and by the time he reads the postcard from Arromanches and argues with his concierge, a lifetime of companionship has vanished. For the captain the family pets were always the most tragic. Dogs, cats, mice, rabbits, lizards, fish even; in his time he had swept up a zoo's worth of cremation. He remembers a pair of pigeons in the twelfth, huddled together, claws still curled around their perch, no more than lumps of cinder. The captain might have stumbled into the ruins of Pompeii rather than an old widow's suicide.

He turns the baker back toward the stairs. Best you stay out of harm's way, monsieur, till the boys have mopped up.

He watches as the man manages a few steps before slumping against the railing. Take your time, monsieur. It's all quite a shock, I know, but consider yourself lucky. You could have been at home.

Emile Notre-Dame unfolded his newspaper, taking care not to reveal the front page, and smoothed the crease through his fingers. A stretch of his arms, a snap of the paper, a determined lick of his thumb. He turned the issue around.

Filling the front page: a man in military uniform clutches at his chest as he falls against the rear seat of an open automobile. Splatters of red ink stain his white tunic; his medals jostle, his helmet is knocked askew. A woman in an elegant day dress and matching feathered hat clings to the man as he falls. In her effort to steady her companion she too loses her balance. There is a look of surprise on her face. Lining the street and crowded on balconies, onlookers stare in disbelief, their stunned expressions and pointing fingers drawn to something at the margin of the illustration.

Monsieur followed the crowd's eyes.

A man in a dark suit leaps from the crowd, his face obscured by the brim of his hat. He waves a small pistol at the couple in the automobile. The weapon spouts a flash of yellow and a soft puff of smoke.

Octavio emerged from the bakery and sat next to his father. He began whistling an unrecognizable tune. After a moment he released as loud a sigh as he could.

You promised, Papa.

Monsieur, suddenly aware he was not alone, glanced from his son to the page and back again. So I did, he said.

Monsieur looked to the sky, scratched his head, ran a finger around his collar. Warm today, he said. Octavio only nodded, his one eyebrow cocked higher still.

That is not a beginning, Papa.

Quite right, Monsieur said. Sometimes a story needs a push to get started. But I know a game. I suppose now is as good a time as any for you to learn.

I like games, Octavio said.

Monsieur explained the rules. First we need a picture, he said. Any one will do. We each pick out a detail, something small and unimportant, and describe what we see. But—and this is the secret—we must use as few words as possible. We take turns, back and forth, a word here, two or three there. Before you know it we have a story.

Who goes first, Papa?

You do.

Monsieur unveiled the front page of the newspaper, his fingers discreetly hiding a murderer. Octavio examined the illustration.

Red spots, he said.

Tomato soup, said his father.

Drips.

A small spoon.

On a big belly.

A big laughing belly.

Laughing so hard.

The soldier falls over.

While his pretty wife.

Tries to catch him.

He is too heavy. All those tomatoes.

She is too skinny. Not enough soup.

The crowd shouts hurrah.

What a show.

Lieutenant Sloppy—

and Madame Hungry.

Driving in their automobile.

An automobile race.

The fastest on four wheels.

Off to find more soup.

And a bigger spoon.

The following day Monsieur Notre-Dame told his son to open the doors for business. The morning's first customers had already formed an unruly line outside the bakery. The small crowd pushed past Octavio, the gossips among them shouting over each other.

Have you seen them!

Murdered!

In broad daylight!

The Austrians won't stand for it!

The Serbs will catch it now!

Russia will jump in!

Watch out for the Germans then!

At precisely 9:16, Monsieur Grenelle squeezed into the bakery. A bachelor who lived two floors below the Notre-Dames, Grenelle spent his days tinkering with watches and clocks. He chose his usual order—two brioche—by peering through his thick spectacles and sliding a callused finger down the glass case. Octavio took up his position: following the finger, removing the chosen buns, lifting the order to his mother waiting behind the till. The boy looked through the case at the sagging knees in the fellow's trousers. Grenelle's head appeared from above, his eyes magnified through his spectacles like blinking balloons. Everyone called him Blind Grenelle.

Quickly, young fellow, he said. Bag them before the Kaiser shows up.

Grenelle smiled.

Meanwhile talk in the shop continued in hushed tones. It was scandalous what a newspaper would print these days and the archduke and his wife well it certainly was a tragedy no matter what you think of their country and if it comes to war well then the eighth will be ready even if the politicians are not and those damned Boche can send us their worst and by God they will meet our best and be all the sorrier for it.

Monsieur's pictures had always been of worlds out of his reach, comings and goings and people and places that had little to do with his own life. Troubles, even when they happened in the city, seemed to be far away. Listening to the chatter in the bakery only reminded him that he had worries of his own. His son was becoming more like him with each passing day.

Even more so with the boy out of school. And try as she might to pull herself from her moods, his wife had become a woman he barely recognized. They both needed him and now this soup-splattered soldier had arrived on his doorstep. Monsieur knew his customers were right: every man in the eighth would be expected to do his duty. He looked at his wife and son. But my duty is here, he mumbled.

Our very best, someone shouted. Even our brave thin baker.

Monsieur Notre-Dame swallowed hard.

If the Lady France calls, he said.

Notre-Dame is it? Like the cathedral?

Monsieur took the recruiting clerk's pen and scratched *N-D*, as though he were marking a country loaf for the ovens.

Having left his wife to mind the bakery, he hurried back to the cake-slice. But instead of striding through the blue doors, a fearless poilu now, he crept unnoticed into the building from a rear laneway.

Grenelle looked up from a stubborn hairspring, unsure whether he had heard the knock at his door or not. He seldom had visitors, once in a while a neighbour with a slow minute hand. He expected no one this day. He paused before turning the latch, took off his spectacles and put his better eye against the peephole.

I'm not sure Madame is up to this, Monsieur said after Grenelle had let him in. The bachelor sensed the shame as it bent his baker's shoulders.

But are *you* up to it, monsieur?

Did you—join up? the baker said.

I tried the mechanized division. Wonderful things these motor cars; practically drive themselves, so I'm told. The recruiting fellow took one look at my spectacles and laughed me into the street. He said they didn't need someone making a wrong turn and ending up in the English Channel.

Grenelle forced a smile. Monsieur only looked at his feet.

I don't how to ask you this.

Of course I will, Grenelle said. It would be an honour to serve a fighting man.

But I haven't asked you anything.

Well now that you know the answer, it should be an easy question.

Will you keep an eye on things, on my wife and boy? I'll worry less if I know a friend is watching out for them. I'll be home as soon as I can.

As I said, an honour. But even honour comes at a cost, my friend.

I don't understand, Monsieur said.

An extra brioche should do it, Grenelle said. Added to my usual order. Free, of course. For that you can stay away until they make you a general.

The morning his regiment was due to report, Monsieur cinched the belt in his uniform trousers to its last hole, floundered inside his infantry coat, straightened his tag number 6694, and descended to the bakery. He snapped a salute and announced to all that their loyal Notre-Dame, freshly scrubbed and polished, would not be away long. Passing among his customers, pumping arms and kissing cheeks, he saw his son standing at the doorway, the boy's hand stiff and proper in its own salute. Monsieur took hold of the boy's elbows. After a few grunting attempts he hoisted his son onto his shoulders.

Not to worry, Monsieur said. We've seen the pictures in our paper, haven't we? So many of us marching off that the trains are full, like a regular August holiday. The army has even hired taxis to chauffeur us all to the front. So it's off for a drive in the country to meet the noisy neighbours and home before you know it with a German goose under my coat. At last, the fattest baker in all Paris.

Monsieur lowered his son to the floor. He gave the counter a swipe with his sleeve, wiped a smudge from his boot and embraced his wife long enough to bring a blush to her cheeks. Madame dug her fingers into the rough fabric of his coat, feeling for his bony shoulders. She whispered in his ear.

I am lost now. Come home and find me.

She knew she would see no letters from her husband.

With two pairs of thin legs pumping high and out of sync, father and son marched into a blistering summer sun. Blind Grenelle stood on the cobbles outside. He bowed as the Notre-Dames passed, a finger to the side of his nose.

Monsieur turned and began marching backwards, his arms waving back and forth as though conducting an orchestra.

It is all numbers and legs, he shouted. Keep the feet moving, one two one two. They will take you anywhere, left right left right. Across the Rhine, three four three four. And back with Christmas dinner, left, right, left, right.

A gentleman on a café terrace gestures for the waiter and then throws his mangled newspaper into the street. Dropping his money on the tray, the man does not notice the young woman stepping over the discarded paper as she hurries past.

In a small park a line of giddy children stretches across the path, waiting for the carousel to open. As the young woman makes her way through the line, she overhears one of the children mention a circus strongman. With one hand! the little girl squeals, her friends sputtering into fits of laughter.

On a bench nearby, two women read copies of the same book. One suddenly closes hers and elbows her friend. Did I not tell you? she says. I knew he had done it. Knew it from page one.

The pair looks up to see the young woman rush past. They return to their reading.

Another block and the young woman stops to catch her breath. She waits for a gap in the crush of automobiles circling the roundabout.

The Pont des Arts was no less boisterous for the wild-fire rumours coming from foreign parts. Crowds of people crossed the iron span as if they were on some sort of perpetual mechanism, their only destination one end of the bridge or the other; their only worry that they might trip over their feet as they changed direction.

Henri Fournier turned his back to the flowing crowd and leaned against the railing. He worked up a mouthful of saliva. Slouching beside him, his friend Mabillon, a fellow son of the trade.

Father thinks the war will be over in a month, Mabillon said.

Henri took aim at a passing barge. He squeezed out a thread of spit and wiped his chin.

What does your father know? He's a bookseller.

The spit vanished in the churning wake of the barge. Mabillon examined a cloud passing overhead.

What's wrong with being a bookseller? Your father is, my father is. You will be, I will be. Such is life.

Henri looked to the stalls lining the quay. He brought his father into focus, fat even at that distance, surrounded by a circle of browsers and gesturing with his hands.

Bookseller, he said. I hope not. There's no money in it.

He leaned his back against the railing and turned to his friend.

Think you'll join up?

Mabillon looked upstream toward the cathedral. A river taxi sat low in the water, smoke swirling from its funnel. The boat was jammed with people clutching hats, pointing fingers, consulting guidebooks.

Doubt it, Mabillon said. Too short. A few centimetres taller and I might pass for eighteen. You?

Henri pressed his spectacles against his face.

Doubt it, he said. Bad eyes.

———

A man in a threadbare sweater and wearing fingerless gloves stepped from the passing crowd and stopped at the railing opposite Henri and Mabillon. The man, tall and sickly pale, gazed downstream, then dropped the carpetbag he was carrying. He pulled a bundle of sticks from the bag. With a swirl of his arms he unfolded an artist's easel, spreading the legs and nudging them into position. A small canvas appeared from the bag. A box of paints, a jar of water and a handful of brushes came next. The man placed the canvas on the easel, stepped back and looked into the distance. After a moment he selected a brush and made a few cautious strokes.

August was not a month for wearing gloves, thought Henri. He wondered how the jar had left the bag without spilling a drop.

Father says the Germans can't swim, Mabillon said. They'll have a hell of a time trying to cross the Rhine.

As the painter added the outlines of the buildings along the quay, the river taxi chugged toward the bridge. Mabillon leaned against the railing next to his friend. They watched the painter construct a sky: layers of grey upon blue upon grey. Watery trails ran down the canvas.

Mabillon turned to watch the taxi approach the bridge.

Henri saw the greenish squares of bookstalls emerge on the canvas, shaded by the blobs of trees.

Mabillon filled his mouth with spit.

Henri turned, crossed his arms on the railing and rested his chin on his hands. What does your father know, he said.

Mabillon jerked his body against the railing. A white glob arced out over the river and broke apart in the breeze. Henri shrugged and put his forehead on his hands. Through the gaps in the bridge's wooden planks, he saw the taxi pass unharmed beneath his feet.

Beside the roundabout a woman folds a stool while a boy packs a row of chipped teapots into a suitcase. He places a handwritten card, 5 *centimes thank you*, in the case and shuts the lid. There is a pause in the traffic and the young woman steps from the curb.

Passing a church, she notices a bent old fellow sitting on the front steps. A bible lies in his lap, a gnarled finger marking a page. By the look of his red-rimmed eyes, she knows the man has been weeping. Her throat tightens. She remembers reading to herself, how it had kept the loneliness at bay.

He healeth the broken in heart, and bindeth up their wounds.
But time presses. She cannot stop.

Rank after rank of soldiers, awkward in stiff uniforms and double-skip strides as they struggled to keep in step, marched the boulevards. A grand show, daily performances, each joyful parade bound for the trains and taxis that would carry them off. Tricolours that had been packed away a month earlier were unfolded and re-hung from railings, children lifted on shoulders startled the horses of the cavalry regiments, young women offered flowers to passing lovers. Old men steadied themselves on their canes, blank stares betrayed dark memories.

August 1914: the city seemed to empty out; the boulevards finally fell silent. As though waiting.

Madame Notre-Dame stood in front of the cellar ovens, her arms folded across an apron dusted in flour, her eyes following thin trails of steam escaping around the oven doors. The first lot of baguettes had gone in. She breathed heavily, impatient for smells she would know as well as her own odour, those fresh-baked aromas that had clung to Emile even as he crawled into bed each night. The rising heat in the cellar became oppressive, the air too thick to breathe. Madame staggered and caught herself as she slumped against the marble table.

The past days pressed down on her. She had watched her husband and son march out of the bakery. She wanted so much to run after them, to take her son's hand and hold him back, to tell him to be as brave as his father. Imagine eating that goose, she would have said. But it was Madame Lafrouche who had caught up with Octavio.

She had spent the previous night writing out every recipe she could remember. The sourdoughs, the croissants, the herbed brioche. She checked and rechecked the cellar stores: the bins of flour, the number of eggs, how much starter was left. She mixed two mounds of baguette dough before she thought her Emile might approve of the proportions. She left a third batch to proof and went upstairs, waking Octavio and telling him to wait for her in the shop. Exhausted now, she realized that she could not keep the bakery going on her own.

A crouched figure, silhouetted against the early-morning light, appeared at the cellar window. Blind Grenelle tapped on the glass and shouted. He said he was reporting as ordered.

In the shop Octavio had fallen back to sleep behind the counter. As Madame nudged the boy, she looked up at Grenelle and asked him why on earth was he standing in the shop at this hour. Had he lost his sense of time with all this war madness? And just who had done the ordering?

Grenelle thought fast.

No one—not even you madame—can make all the breads then run upstairs and sell them—which is not to say that you are weak or infirm—in fact quite the contrary madame—but would it not be easier—if you had some help in that regard—not the baking of course—the selling I mean—after all how hard could it be—taking someone's money and handing them a loaf—which does not imply that your work in the shop has ever been easy—I only meant that you and Emile were such good partners—and it would be a shame if things floundered in his absence—I mean to say—that someone—with a bit of knowledge as to how things work—who knows most of the customers—could even manage the one-franc key—might help out upstairs—mind the boy you understand—leave the important work to an expert—such as yourself madame—and by the way have you heard—the government is banning croissants—something to do with the city's supply of butter—but of course you would know this already—

He concluded with a yawn. My apologies, madame. It is very early.

It was my husband, wasn't it.

He only meant well, madame.

Madame brushed the front of her apron. I have no doubt he did. Then so be it. We will be easier to watch over if you are here. I take it you have never made a proper loaf of bread?

No, madame.

Then you can mind the shop. Thankfully my boy has a head for numbers, he'll help you settle in. In the meantime, I'll thank you to stay out of my cellar.

Grenelle put his arm around Octavio's shoulder. The pair stood at attention.

We shall not fail you, Grenelle said.

Madame thanked him for the news about the croissants.

One less thing to worry about, she said.

———

The customers were patient with Grenelle's apprenticeship, forgave him his confusions over who had selected the sourdough and how many loaves of rye—I assure you mademoiselle they will be ready at any moment—were due out of the ovens. A few of the gossips moaned about the wait, or the incorrect price, or the forgotten change, but Octavio would step in and whisper in Grenelle's ear.

Pay them no mind, monsieur, they always complain.

Near the Métro the young woman pauses for a moment to watch as a man, perhaps her own age, appears from nowhere and greets a lady friend. He hesitates, then leans in to kiss her cheeks. She seems unsure in a pair of new shoes; she nervously fingers her hair. The man's face gleams with sweat. Tugging at the short legs of his trousers, he offers her a bouquet of drooping flowers. She smiles as she accepts them. The young woman looks away and walks on.

More than four years of rumours and speculations, anxious headlines and invented illustrations, half-truths and certain lies flowed around the Boulangerie Notre-Dame. This sea of war would lap at the bakery's doorstep or lift itself as black walls, threatening to drown all within. But inevitably to pass, leaving bits of hearsay and fact in its wake as it radiated from a distant storm.

What Madame Notre-Dame would remember of those years, or what others hoped she might remember, were the politicians reinstating the making of croissants. She would come to produce her own version, a fine balance of butter and dough, and no one would fault her for showing them off to her husband were he ever to return.

She might have remembered the evenings spent helping her son organize the growing pile of newspapers he was saving for his father, or the Sunday when Octavio would teach Blind Grenelle the story game. It was the first Christmas of the war: the two of them on the front step shivering in the cold and mimicking an illustration of soldiers huddled around a trench fire. They were a happy group, the poilu on the front page, a few of them singing, one fellow enjoying a pipe and a steaming mug, a pair dancing what appeared to be a jig.

Or she might have remembered the knot loosening in her stomach as she pictured her Emile, warm and safe like the scene in the newspaper; or as she stood watch at the top of the cake-slice, her son and Grenelle linking elbows and twirling across the cobbles below.

What Madame Lafrouche would remember was 1916. Soldiers returning to Paris on leave, but not her Alphonse. Hollow men slumped in doorways, broken men struggling with new crutches. But no sign of Alphonse. The postman knocking at her door that summer; the way he took off his cap and wiped the sweat from his forehead as he handed her the telegram. The word that had hovered over the eighth since the winter: *Verdun.* Then the instructions as to where Madame might find her husband's resting place, once the fighting had moved on and the army could arrange suitable memorial plots. She would remember the darkness of that summer and the mad hope that the army had made a mistake. Most of all she would remember the pain in Madame Notre-Dame's eyes, worrying that her own man had met such a fate, and Grenelle's quiet reassurance to the baker's wife. No news is good news, he had whispered.

Blind Grenelle would remember the spring of 1918. Bread finally rationed. Everyone now complaining, standing in day-long queues for meagre allotments, that such privation meant a slow and certain death for the country's soul. He would remember the low thudding of heavy guns outside the city, the catch in people's throats as they talked of the enemy massing on the outskirts, the story he conjured to distract Octavio as news of bombs landing in the city spread through the shop. Pay no attention, he told the boy. That is our army, not theirs. Our boys are setting off fireworks, practising for when victory comes. Imagine the celebration we will have when your father marches through those doors.

———

Octavio would remember his tenth birthday, August 1918, and his mother asking him for a story. Something from your book, she said. He was stunned. He ran up the spiral staircase to the attic and returned with the *Arabian Nights*, opening it to the picture of a man in a turban and elegant robes riding a flying horse. He couldn't tell the same story he and his father had told each other. He wanted something special for his mother, she had never asked for a story before. This is one of Papa's horses, he said, knowing how she would reply. But your father hasn't got any horses, she said. Is he hiding them, somewhere in the cellar perhaps? Octavio chuckled. That would be silly, he said. No, Maman, this horse is one of the kings who pulled the cart delivering Papa's marble. I see, she said, pretending to be surprised. And who is the fellow riding this Louis?

Octavio would remember his response. That is Papa. Flying over the war and on his way home.

What a birthday present that would be, Madame said.

And then the final November. There had been murmurs for weeks. The city vibrated with them, daily, almost hourly.

Madame was sitting in the cellar, flour dusting her arms white, her face glowing in the heat, her back feeling the first chills of winter seeping through the old stone walls farthest from the oven doors. In this lull after the day's first rush of customers she tried, as she had every morning since Emile had turned the corner that afternoon four years earlier, to remember his face. The silly grin as he marched backwards and out of sight. The picture had gone soft now, more a flicker than anything she might reach out and hold. Lately she had begun working herself into fits of panic as she imagined a bullet thumping into her husband's chest, or a table where a doctor was frantically trying to stop his bleeding, or him stumbling along a stretch of road, all alone, the trees on either side blown to stumps.

It was then she heard the bells of Saint-Augustin.

On a Monday? Madame thought.

The sounds of running footsteps came next, on the street outside the cellar window. There were muffled shouts. She couldn't make out what they were saying. She thought she heard singing. The shop's floorboards above her head began creaking more than usual. Something was going on upstairs.

As she moved toward the stairs, Octavio's face appeared at the top.

Come quick, Maman. It is all true. The war is over. Papa is coming home.

By noon Madame Notre-Dame was elbowing her way through drunken, dancing streets to the war department.

She stood in a long queue of women. When she reached the counter Madame informed a small man that she had heard nothing from her husband since the war began. The clerk moved his bottle of brandy to one side, asked a few questions, scribbled notes in a ledger, explained the unfairness of the tens of thousands of such cases and the handful of clerks assigned to resolve them. He advised that patience and celebration were the order of the day, madame; the matter would be looked into. In the meantime did she care to join him in a toast to peace?

Day after day, Madame would close the bakery during the afternoon lull and return to the war department. The queue outside, the hundreds of wives and girlfriends and mothers and children huddled in hope, would only grow longer.

The young woman turns a corner and bumps into a rag picker, knocking into the gutter the three hats the old woman wears. Her cart is overflowing with clothes. The young woman apologizes and bends to pick up the hats, no worse for their fall.

There is no need to rush, mademoiselle, the old woman says. Her voice softens. Whatever you are late for, my dear, will still be there when you arrive.

The letter came months later, the return address a hospital near Amiens.

—your husband has been under our care. He was discovered some two years ago now, starving in the ruins of a village near here. How he had managed to survive in the cellar of a bombed-out bakery we will never know. When he was brought to us he barely spoke. He seemed not to hear when we asked him to write his name. For a while we thought he might have gone deaf, what with the shelling you understand.

Apart from his tag number we have had no way of knowing who he is or where he came from. We sent letter after letter to the war department inquiring about our brave number 6694. Just imagine our pleasure at finally learning his name. Be at peace, madame, knowing your man is well and whole if still very thin. His voice has returned and he tells us the most remarkable stories. We are further pleased to inform you he will shortly be returned to you by train. We shall miss our Emile Notre-Dame, infantry first-class. He has been a most cooperative patient and has lightened our burden through these dreadful years.

Soldiers crowded the station platform, shuffling into ragged formation, their faces unshaven, dirty, old before their time. Madame clutched the letter, searching each blank stare as the men marched past, their double ranks parting around her. Emile Notre-Dame was not among them. When she realized she was alone on the platform, she began to panic, her hands trembling as she unfolded the letter and read for the hundredth time the hospital's instructions regarding the train from Amiens.

Madame saw him from the corner of her eye. Monsieur Notre-Dame stood under the station clock, fidgeting with the one remaining button of his tunic. Had she not turned her head she would have passed him altogether, another soiled uniform in a grimy ocean pouring off the trains. His face had gone as white as cotton, his eyes shrunk into his head; streaks of grey ran through his shaggy hair. His trousers hung from him as though he were a boy playing in his father's clothes. A stamped square of paper—*Paris 8ᵉ*—had been pinned to his chest.

Madame stepped in front of her husband, her eyes searching to meet his. She reached for his face.

Monsieur let go of the button and looked up. A smile was slow to appear.

I am sorry, mademoiselle, he said. I was looking for someone.

You were looking for me, Madame said.

The grey in his eyes caught the light. Then you must be the Lady France. I am your servant, madame.

He struggled to bow from the waist.

Octavio watched a man who looked like his father slump into a chair. He couldn't make sense of it. He tried starting a story. Home, he said. His father didn't respond. He felt his face grow hot. He couldn't stop himself from pulling on his father's sleeve.

But, Papa. This is wrong! Home! With a goose under your coat, you said. You would be the fattest baker in all Paris! You're not fat at all. Where are your medals? It was all numbers and legs, you said. Onetwothreefour.

I saved your newspapers and I was good! I helped Maman. It's not fair, Papa!

Octavio felt his eyes filling with tears. You promised, Papa. You promised a Christmas goose.

Madame took hold of her boy's hands. Go and find Grenelle, she said.

Grenelle cleaned his spectacles and waited for his eyes to adjust to the dim of the shop.

Octavio wiped his runny nose on his sleeve. Maman has tried all she can, he said. Papa doesn't want to eat. I brought him one of his papers. He wasn't interested in that either. I think we need help, monsieur.

Monsieur had fallen asleep where he sat, his uniform covered in crumbs. A newspaper lay across his lap. Grenelle told Octavio to open the curtains, then asked where his mother was.

Octavio moved from window to window. Upstairs, he said.

Sunlight poured into the shop, stirring the sleeping baker. Monsieur jolted upright, his gaunt face twisted in fear.

Welcome home, my friend, Grenelle said. Wouldn't you be more comfortable upstairs?

Monsieur's eyes darted back and forth as though he had been struck blind.

Safer in the cellar, he said, a hand digging into his trouser pocket, searching for a watch Grenelle knew was long lost.

Monsieur looked outside. Any minute now. The guns will start. We are dead men if we stay here.

Grenelle turned to Octavio. We'll need a blanket and something for his head, he said.

In the cellar Grenelle fashioned a bed on the table in front of the ovens. Octavio brushed away a few nuggets of hard dough and flour dust. I was born on this table, he said.

Then if it is good enough for babies, Grenelle said, it is good enough for their fathers.

Helping the baker to his feet took little effort. The thinnest for certain now, Grenelle thought, guiding the man down the narrow stairs into the cellar. Monsieur curled himself on the marble table. Octavio pulled the blanket over his father's shoulder.

Grenelle left the cake-slice and returned within the hour, carrying a wheel of cheese, a tin of sardines and a few bits of fruit in a string bag. Lunch for the four of us, he said. He asked if Madame had come down at all.

Octavio went to the rear of the building, stood on the bottom step and called up the stairwell, straining to hear the scrape of chair legs, the shuffle of feet. There was none. He returned to the bakery. She must be very tired, he said.

We'll keep the bakery closed for now, Grenelle said. Everyone is tired.

That night Octavio lay on the floor under the table and his snoring father, the cake-slice creaking and moaning above them. Drifting in and out of sleep, he thought he heard footsteps on the stairs. Our Lady Herself then appeared at the cellar door, her glowing hands holding a tray heaped with pains au chocolat. Octavio rolled over. The dream faded as Mary spread her arms and smiled.

Blind Grenelle sat in a corner of one of the shop windows. Knees pulled to his chin, head lolling against his arms, he fought the exhaustion clouding his head. He wanted to stay awake; dawn would come soon enough. He imagined various excuses and apologies, ones he would tell in quiet tones when he peeked out from the blue doors and greeted the day's first customers. I know how much we'd like matters to get back to normal, he would say, and Madame has asked me to thank you all for your concern. It's been quite a journey for our baker. There's much catching up to do. We'll just leave them alone for a day or two, shall we? Let them get reacquainted. I am sure you understand.

—

By noon the next day Madame had still not come down to the bakery. Grenelle told Octavio to keep an eye on his father. I'll go upstairs to fetch a few things from my place, he said. Back in no time.

Grenelle reached the top-floor landing. The door to the Notre-Dame apartment was open. He called out to Madame. He could hear something coming from the bedroom. He stepped inside and called again.

He found Madame sitting at the side of the bed and staring into nothing. Grenelle's first thought as he saw her swollen eyes and raw cheeks was that she hadn't stopped crying since yesterday. In front of her the armoire door was ajar, wedged against the bed.

Madame? Grenelle said.

Leave me alone.

Why don't you come downstairs. I'll make us some coffee.

Madame turned to the blind watchmaker.

I wanted to change, you see. Wear something nice. To welcome him home. But I couldn't move the bed. Now I've gone and jammed the drawer and—

Let me help you, Grenelle said.

—now it's too late. I don't think Emile will notice anyway.

I'm sure he will, Madame. He simply needs time to adjust.

Please go away.

If you'll allow me, Grenelle said.

Madame finally screamed at the blind watchmaker.

As you wish, Madame. I'll come back later.

Grenelle gently closed the bedroom door behind him.

Late afternoon the following day. Grenelle checked his watch. It had been another twenty-four hours. Or more, by his reckoning, and still Madame had shut herself away. He was about to leave the shop and go upstairs when a uniform appeared at the bakery doors.

The police inspector explained the reason for his visit.

I know the Notre-Dames, Grenelle said. Monsieur is not well and Madame is not yet awake. You may leave your report with me.

The inspector said it was most irregular and he was behind in his rounds and had a full morning of notices to deliver but under the circumstances he would be on his way and please express the department's condolences and have a pleasant day monsieur goodbye.

In the cellar, Grenelle pulled the report close to his face, searching for the focus. He cleared his throat, and began to read aloud.

It is this officer's duty to record that one Madame Immacolata Notre-Dame, lately of the eighth district, was pronounced dead at thirteen minutes after two o'clock yesterday morning, in the vicinity of the Church of Saint-Augustin, having succumbed to grievous injuries suffered while being trampled by a horse which was engaged at the time of the incident in pulling the delivery wagon of one Monsieur Philippe Lecler, resident of Courbevoie, eel monger and documented owner of the aforementioned animal. Despite a variety of testimonies regarding the moonless night and the resulting blackness, the weight of the eels, the momentum of the wagon, as well as the victim's observed agitation and depressed physical nature at the time, testimonies that were duly obtained during an exhaustive examination of the scene and through notarized eyewitness accounts, as included herewith, the incident was determined by this officer to be an unavoidable and unfortunate accident. No further action was deemed necessary and the aforementioned Monsieur Lecler, having been declared by this officer innocent of any negligence or wrongdoing, was permitted to return to his residence with the animal and cart in question. Signed and dated et cetera.

Grenelle looked up from his reading. Monsieur had said nothing. Apart from one eyebrow cocked a little higher than the other, there was no expression on Octavio's face. As though the watchmaker had been speaking a foreign language.

Searching Monsieur's face for any sign of understanding, Grenelle could only find what was in his own mind's eye. Madame gathering her shawl around her head. Finding a dark gap between the street lamps. Waiting for Lecler's old mare to gather speed. Timing her step off the curb. Closing her eyes.

Monsieur smiled. He asked if anyone would like a story.

He has been in there a long time, someone says. Do you think he is all right?

Would you be? comes a reply.

The crowd assures itself that with the brigade already at work, the baker is in the best hands he can be.

Heads tilt back as the brigade appears amid the ruins of the top floor of the cake-slice. One or two of the younger firemen forget themselves, wave their helmets and puff their chests, roll their shirtsleeves to pump sooty muscled arms. A few in the crowd, eager to be characters in a dangerous tale of city life they will tell their disbelieving country relatives, forget themselves and wave in return.

Grenelle stooped to pick up the flowers that had begun to accumulate on the bakery's doorstep. Madame Lafrouche approached, in her hand a red carnation. I believe they were a favourite of hers, she said.

Certainly the colour, Grenelle said.

How is the boy?

Good days and bad, madame. Like yourself, I suspect.

Madame Lafrouche drew a deep breath. My Alphonse—yes—two years ago now—feels like yesterday—loved his sourdough—sorry—yes—the boy—you say he is well?

He will be, madame. He is a strong boy. It is a great comfort to his father.

Are they reading his book? Madame said. It was a gift, you know—Alphonse's idea of course—still—

Grenelle took the carnation from the woman's hand. A lie would do no harm, he thought. They read it every day, madame.

Madame Lafrouche wrung her hands. This may not be—the right time—but I was wondering—if—when—the bakery might open again. It would lighten all our burdens.

Soon, Grenelle said, soon. And you are right to ask, madame. It would be good to return to normal. I will see that Monsieur gets your flower.

The Boulangerie Notre-Dame had managed on meagre supplies for much of the war. It was the city's good fortune that apart from brief restrictions on butter, there had never been an outright loss of essentials. The display case sat half empty most of the time—Madame had kept the varieties of breads to a minimum—but customers of the Boulangerie Notre-Dame had never gone truly hungry.

I am a pilgrim in a strange land, Grenelle thought as

he leaned against the marble table and tried to make sense of what remained of the stores. Octavio pulled himself up and sat on the table. Grenelle turned to the boy.

Your father was always bragging about his apprentice. That Octavio has the gift, he would say, a Notre-Dame through and through. So how gifted are you, exactly?

Octavio shrugged. Papa let me work at the ovens sometimes, he said. I helped him with the easy breads. We would make brioche all the time.

Not your mother's brioche, I hope, Grenelle said.

No, monsieur, Papa's special variety. The one with the herbs.

Octavio looked over at his father and smiled. Monsieur Notre-Dame was sitting in his corner of the cellar, staring up at the window.

Those I have missed, Grenelle said.

Dumping flour, yeast and water into a bowl was easy enough; it required no more than a dozen tries before Octavio and Grenelle thought the portions of salt and sugar looked correct. The boy thought hard to remember his father's way with the eggs: the graceful toss, like a juggler, from one hand to the other; the tentative tap against the rim of the bowl, the final swift and sure blow. By his fifth attempt, Octavio had found the miraculous force: opening the egg against the rim of the bowl, letting the contents drip into the mixture, keeping the shell in his hands. By the seventh egg he managed the process one-handed. With the tenth and eleventh he could crack an egg in each hand.

Your father's son, Grenelle said.

Mixing became a struggle, the watchmaker cursing as more dough stuck to his fingers than stayed in the bowl. Octavio climbed on the marble table. On his knees he pushed and pulled at the dough until his wrists ached. Grenelle stood by, tossing flour across the table, dropping in handfuls of butter. They finally produced a glistening globe of dough. Grenelle, covered in flour, and Octavio, panting and red-faced, stared at their creation as though it were about to explode.

Monsieur suddenly rose from his corner. Unsteady on his legs, he gripped the edge of the table. My marble, he said.

Octavio and Grenelle looked up at Monsieur's beaming face.

Did you know, gentlemen, that it was cut in the quarries of Tuscany? A slab as tall as the cake-slice. Shipped across a sea broiling with sharks and mermaids, you know, and loaded onto a fire-breathing train, non-stop, to the banks of the Seine. They winched it onto a barge rowed by a hundred men. A full day before it entered the city. It was hoisted to a cart pulled by five stallions named for kings, four Henris and a Louis. From the quayside to here you could hear twenty hooves shaking the cobblestones from their mortar. And now here it sits, *mia bella Italiana*, waiting for my dough.

As he spoke Monsieur made a circular motion with his hands, rolling an invisible ball between his palms.

Grenelle began pulling handfuls of dough. He followed Monsieur's movements, rolling each handful smooth in his own hands. Octavio found the brioche trays. Each lump became a ball; each ball was tucked in its mould in the trays. The glaze, Octavio said.

He broke an egg into another bowl, added a splash of water. With the softest of strokes, remembering how his father would guide his hand, Octavio painted the top of each ball of dough with a golden wash.

He pointed to a jar tucked in the cellar's rafters. Papa's secret, he whispered.

Grenelle placed the jar on the table; the smell of rosemary filled his nostrils. Octavio scooped out a fistful. Hovering over the trays, he rubbed the dried herb between his hands. A dusting of green flakes fell, like the softest snow, across the little jewels of bread.

———

Fourteen minutes, thirty-two seconds, Grenelle said. He slid the trays of brioche onto the table: two dozen domes, some perfectly round, others deflated and burnt, all tinged with a hint of green.

Can you hear them? Monsieur said.

Octavio fumbled a brioche between his hands until it cooled. He held it to his father's ear. The boy tapped the bread with his thumb. Monsieur grinned.

They sang, you know. The mermaids. With my marble sailing over them.

The next morning the Please Call Again sign was gone from the windows of the Boulangerie Notre-Dame. Madame Lafrouche was among the first to be served.

There were nights when Octavio would lie under the table in the cellar, listening as the oven doors shed their heat, their metallic ticks mingled with his father's snores as the baker drifted into sleep.

Monsieur would talk in his slumber, mumbling about dry boots or warm blankets or trees that still threw shade. Octavio would then tiptoe out of the cellar and climb the stairs to the apartment at the top of the cake-slice. He would pull one of the under-stuffed chairs to the window and watch the street below.

The street was so narrow that it seemed always in shadow. Doors and windows became black holes; the surrounding buildings leaned like drunkards. A few figures—night workers, insomniacs, vagrants—would sometimes appear. To Octavio they looked to be nothing more than hats or the tops of heads. The same heads, the same hats, the same umbrellas when it was raining. Octavio thought the darkness was playing tricks: black shapes emerged from doorways and disappeared around a corner, only to tiptoe their way back to their doorways, wait for him to fall asleep, then repeat the process. The hats, the heads, the umbrellas seemed always to be leaving, never returning.

Octavio had never ventured farther from the bakery than his school. Now, watching the street from the top of the cake-slice, he wondered where everyone went as they vanished around the corner. His hands grew clammy at the thought of walking away from the bakery's front step.

As the first streaks of morning lightened the sky, a rag woman might appear, her cart heaped with blankets, old coats, bedsheets, curtains, quilts, hats, shoes, gloves, stockings, dresses, trousers. She was a bundle of rags herself: layer on layer, socks over shoes, stockings over socks, skirts on top of trousers, scarves over coats over jackets over sweaters over vests over shirt. On her head she balanced a few hats, each brim narrower than the one beneath. The old woman would step into the light under each street lamp, then glide from one lamp to the next, disappearing only to re-appear, eventually to reach the corner and be gone.

Octavio had no wish to follow any of them: the night wanderers, the rag woman. The thought of leaving the cake-slice, and what had happened to his mother and father after they left, turned his stomach over and left him in a nervous sweat.

But by then it would be time to get back to the cellar, fire the ovens and wake his father.

A barely visible haze stings the young woman's eyes as she rounds a corner. The smell of smoke fills her nostrils. She pulls up, startled by a mass of people that seems to have risen fully formed out of the cobblestones. She keeps her head down, her hair falling out of her scarf.

No one takes any notice of her as she hovers at the edge of the crowd.

Madame Céleste convinced herself, as any parent might, that the accident had never happened. She gently guided a new dress over young Isabeau's outstretched arms, she patiently directed the girl's fingers as they practised bow after bow in her hair, she smiled and nodded when Isabeau, reading her magazines, would offer a little girl's opinion on this hat or those shoes or that chemise.

In those years her private worries were for Isabeau: that the girl would suffer at the tongues of the boulevard gossips was too much to imagine. The moment they stepped from the Normande apartments, Madame did her best—a stern tone of voice hiding a nervous tremor—to shield her daughter from pointing fingers and cruel stares. You know very well, my dear, that a young woman does not venture out bare-headed. If you insist on coming with me, then for goodness' sake wear a scarf.

Yet as time passed, her daughter's flaw did not fade. The more Madame Céleste tried to ignore it, the more the scar's rawness glared at her. Her fears turned on her. She knew the colder gossips would never again consider the grand Madame Céleste as fashionable, what with that poor burned face peeking out from behind her skirts. None of them would remember *magnificent, magnificent*. She knew they would talk only of her failure. Such a proud mother, they would say, and look at the result. They would never blame Isabeau for her own clumsiness. No, it would be her, the *shameful, shameful* Céleste, who would be condemned. A mother not vigilant enough to protect her own child.

Must we go out today, my dear? The weather looks about to turn.

Isabeau strained into a teenager's ungainly limbs. Her favourite magazines had been folded enough times that they began falling apart at the slightest touch. She moped around the Normande apartments like a graveside mourner. Finally Pascal had had enough.

Perhaps a book might distract her, he suggested to his wife. Her birthday is coming up. Could she have really grown so quickly?

Pascal handed his daughter her gift. It was dog-eared and threadbare, easily tucked in a pocket, a tourist's guide to the Louvre. The bookseller had guaranteed that the book—note the numerous reproductions, monsieur, it is a most rare edition—was worth ten times what he was charging. Pascal's only comment was how dull and small the paintings were. I trust the real things are worth the visit, he said, handing the bookseller half as much.

You won't be disappointed, monsieur.

Returning home, Pascal inscribed the title page.

To our own masterpiece on the occasion of her fourteenth birthday. With love, Maman, Papa and Zouzou.

Isabeau would retreat to her bedroom for hours at a time, curled under the duvet and reading the descriptions in the guide. Studying the museum's floor plans, following dotted-line routes through the galleries with her finger, examining the muddy images. She would argue with herself as her moods swung, choosing the most tragic pictures only to reject them for ones more cheery; drawing little stars beside her favourites, underlining names and adjectives in the descriptions, blacking out others, dreaming how the paintings—her paintings now— might appear were they to hang in her own room.

Her imaginings became a teenager's obsessions. At the supper table she talked of little else. How beautiful her paintings must be. How their subjects must leap from the frames as you walk by, Maman, how their eyes must surely follow you around the gallery. How hundreds of people, like your customers, Papa, must visit the museum every single day.

Please, Papa, may we go too?

One Sunday, Pascal Normande suddenly awoke from his afternoon nap.

We should be seen, he said, rubbing his eyes. Seeing things—

Madame Céleste was pacing, moving vases left then right then back again. Things? she said, running her finger along a windowsill.

—the theatre, Pascal said. Plays, openings, galleries. As we did before—before—

Galleries? Madame said.

Art. The paintings in Isabeau's book, for instance. It would be good for business, don't you think? Mingling again with the clientele. Even Isabeau knows who visits the museums.

Mingling? Herded like sheep, you mean.

Isabeau does love them, Pascal said. How can a father deny his daughter?

You do not mean the three of us would go out?

We cannot hide her forever, my dear.

You cannot be serious.

Our charade has gone on long enough. The girl deserves to be happy.

It is not a charade. It is preservation. Think of the talk if we start parading her around. I could not bear it.

Pascal waved a hand. There is already talk, he said. Did you know we keep Isabeau chained in a cupboard like some sort of wild animal? I have overheard whispers that you yourself threw the boiling water out of jealousy. Trust me, the day after they see that scar they will chatter about something else. Ugliness makes no less fleeting an impression than beauty. Your gossips will not remember Isabeau either way. Besides, they will all be looking at you.

I would rather they didn't, Madame said.

———

Madame Céleste insisted the trees be in full bud, the grounds of the Tuileries dry and easily walked. There would be no wind to disturb a hat or lift a dress or unravel Isabeau's scarf. The skies would be a clear spring blue.

Her scarf? said Pascal.

The child will be wearing pink, Madame said. And one of your scarves, the peacock number, I think. Be certain she remembers how the fold should lie against her cheek, how the ends must flow over the shoulders.

Isabeau pulled her ear away from the keyhole. Her face was burning. The dread of being seen, the staring, the murmurs, seemed to bring her scar to life, crawling across her cheek. But here was her chance. She would risk anything to see her paintings. She looked at her dog.

Zouzou, the Louvre. Can you imagine?

The dog, nearly blind and entirely deaf, nuzzled into a warm spot against Isabeau's ankle.

The Normandes joined the crush of bodies funnelling through a set of narrow doors. The crowd emerged as if sprayed from a hose, dishevelled and wide-eyed into the Grande Galerie.

Isabeau wore her father's scarf, the ends swept over her shoulders and down her back. Clutching her guidebook, staring at the glass ceiling, she stumbled against her mother. Madame Céleste shooed her away, muttering about rushing about and what happened when one was not careful, as she smoothed the drape of her dress.

Light streamed in through the ceiling as if it didn't exist and the gallery were open to the sky. Isabeau put a hand to her forehead, shading her eyes. The end of the hall seemed a thousand miles away. The way it appeared to vanish in the distance caused gooseflesh to climb out of her pink gloves and spread up her arms. She felt a tickle behind her knees, bristles crawling across her scalp. She shuddered at the flutters in her stomach.

Adults swarmed around her. Some leaned in toward the paintings placed at eye level, others bent back to take in those hung to the ceiling. No one noticed when they bumped into the girl with the peacock scarf.

As Isabeau inched along the gallery, there were flashes of colour: paintings she thought she knew, now hardly recognizable in their deep reds and golds, rich greens and yellows, inky blacks and blues. They were all there, her roommates, her favourites, grown gigantic compared to the grainy reproductions in her book. Some paintings stretched from floor to ceiling, their subjects ready, as she knew they would be, to step out of their canvases. The smaller ones—so much smaller than Isabeau had imagined—crowded together, cheek to ear to shoulder. There were decapitated heads on plates, grinning saints pointing skyward, serious men of business, mothers and daughters, bonneted babies, shipwrecked sailors, musicians, goddesses dancing through ancient ruins.

The current of visitors slowed and bunched together, elbowing their way to see a particular painting. Isabeau knew from her floor plans who they had found. It was *La Joconde*. Isabeau had never much cared for her. The reproduction in the guidebook made the woman look as grimy as a street sweeper. Isabeau had read in one of her father's newspapers that someone had actually stolen her a few years back. For months after, thousands had returned to the museum to weep and stare at the faded wallpaper and empty hooks where she had hung. People had even left poems and flowers and letters of condolence, as though the missing woman had been their sweetheart. It was all such nonsense, Isabeau thought. The woman hanging before her now was a chubby lump, her dress was dull, her hair needed washing, and her hands were much too large.

There was someone else Isabeau was looking for. She had always looked out from the guidebook, a girl not much older than Isabeau herself, her eyes pleading not to be crowded around, or pointed at, or worshipped. She was hung amid imagined landscapes and scenes of peasant life. The small plaque beside her read: *422, The Spring, Ingres, signed and dated, 1856.*

Alone in her bedroom Isabeau had given her a few secret names—she was Tethys perhaps, or Iolanthe. Something exotic and otherworldly. But now that they had come face to face, Isabeau thought she looked more of a Sofia. She stood naked at the edge of a glassy pool in a thick green forest, balancing an urn on her shoulder, water dripping through her fingers. Her skin appeared to be lit from within; there were no blotches or freckles. No downy hair under her arms or in her private places. There were no scars.

Isabeau blushed, as though she were looking in her own mirror. Sofia made no move to cover her nakedness, yet Isabeau could see something in her pose, the way the girl's knees tucked against each other. Isabeau pictured two sisters, alone in their own room, sharing the same shyness. Revealing to each other, between their giggles and groans, how their bodies were becoming womanly.

She admired Sofia's face: the lips slightly parted, the beginnings of a cautious smile. Isabeau stepped closer. The girl's eyes were like her own, large and dark, sloped at the corners. Her hair was not quite as chocolate perhaps, but not far off. And she could have been as tall though it was difficult for Isabeau to tell. She tried to see herself and Sofia standing back to back, knocking their heads against each other and laughing.

She would be the brave one, Isabeau thought. Sofia had nothing to hide. But even so, they could be sisters.

The young woman watches the smoke rising from the building across the street. Bits of paper swirl around her. She opens her hand; a few flakes come to rest. She reads the half-words and singed letters, wonders at the flashes of orange and red and green lying in her palm. On her toes, shifting back and forth, she peers between the shoulders of the crowd. In that instant she reads the name of the bakery and recognizes the man stumbling from the building, his familiar suit now covered with ashes.

Octavio and his father spent their Sundays on the bakery step. Octavio would open the day's newspaper, point to an illustration or photograph, suggest a word or two to prompt the game along. Monsieur would only grin or stare blankly at the page or say nothing at all. Octavio would try another. Then without warning Monsieur might launch into a story on his own. One morning a politician's walrus-whiskered face, frowning from the corner of a back page, became the Pope of Avignon.

Now he's a demanding customer, Monsieur said. Impossible to please. If your croissants don't flake to his liking or your crusts aren't firm he will strip you naked and without so much as a Holy Mary Mother of God, tie you to a post in his cloister. He'll hand out palm fronds to your regulars and invite them to take a switch or two to your skinny baker's backside.

Octavio Notre-Dame grew to an able manhood, as slender a baker as his father though a full head taller. Blind Grenelle managed to gain his own notoriety, with customers making requests for what they came to call the Watch Man's Special: a misshapen braid of bread that never appeared quite done but managed to melt in the mouth. The buxom young woman with her wheat, the laughing baker and his aromas, the cherubs with their angelic breakfasts, Our Lady and her beer: all continued their watch over the Boulangerie Notre-Dame.

After sliding the day's third lots into the ovens, Octavio would come up to the shop for a breath of air. A few of the early gossips may have lingered a while, mumbling among themselves, waiting for more attentive ears to turn up once the lunchtime rush began. Nothing much doing out in the world today, someone might announce. We might as well stay put. You never know, something may happen here. Grenelle would shrug and go back to straightening the baskets.

Octavio would lean against the display case and pick bits of flour from under his fingernails.

A silence would settle in as fresh aromas began drifting from the cellar. How about a story then, someone would finally ask. Octavio would scratch his head and flex the kinks out of his back.

The further adventures of the missing N were a favourite subject. Octavio might search his memory of the nuns' geography lessons, then begin by stating that Napoleon had had nothing to do with the disappearance. In fact, Octavio would say, it was the city of Nice that was to blame. He would explain: in a far-off time the citizens had decided to show their civic pride by decorating the doorways of their homes.

Southerners, a gossip would say. Not be trusted, if you ask me.

Maybe not, Octavio continued, but the city fathers thought this was a grand idea and so sent wandering gangs out to lift Is and Cs and Es and of course Ns from wherever they could find them. Try not to murder anyone was the fathers' only request of their ruffians. Even so, not a corner of the country was safe. Villages like Issou, or Courcelles, or even the hamlet of Épretot had their signage vandalized in the middle of the night.

Octavio would pause and hang his head as though in mourning. But poor tiny Nantenne, he would sigh.

Theirs was the greatest loss. An innocent lamb of a village, bloated with its four Ns and two Es, only to be gnawed at by letter-thieving wolves.

And where might this poor tragic Nantenne be, came the inevitable question. Octavio would cover his face, hide his mock tears, and point a quivering finger outside. It is hard to say, my friends. No one knows the way anymore. All the road signs are gone.

Where exactly *is* Nantenne? Octavio asked Grenelle one evening as they locked up. I remember the name from school, but the location escapes me. Grenelle said even he wasn't certain, but as he recalled it may have been on the road to Dijon.

Have you been there? Octavio said.

In my travelling days, Grenelle replied.

It was said that Blind Grenelle had left home at fifteen: an idle boy with nimble fingers and uncanny hearing. He could listen to any mechanical mishap—a skipped gear, a sputtering valve, the gritty scrape of a wheel— and know within seconds how to fix it. Pocket watches were full of such problems. His small work, Grenelle liked to call it.

Grenelle apprenticed for a time, resetting baubles and calibrating clock weights, with a jeweller in Lyon.

After a year he grew tired of toiling for someone else. He fashioned a tool case out of old suitcases, slung it over his shoulder then travelled from town to town offering appraisals, repairs and restorations. He loved the wandering life, the work of gluing gems smaller than a grain of sand, rewinding coils as fine as human hair, polishing a locket to reveal a long-forgotten promise of love. It was suspected in the bakery that there weren't many places Grenelle hadn't been in his time, and a few whispers claimed there weren't many hearts the man hadn't broken along the way. Hard to imagine, the gossips would say, our blind tinker wandering into a village, stringing a broken necklace, smiling a winning smile, caressing an appreciative neck as he re-clasps the chain, finding a dry straw bed in the barn out back, then vanishing before the sun comes up. Hard to imagine, but weren't we all young once?

When Octavio asked if the rumours were true, Grenelle would only smile.

You shouldn't believe all that you hear, my boy, but I have been here and there.

And where, exactly, is that? Octavio said. Here and there.

Here was the place I usually found myself in, Grenelle replied. It wouldn't take long to lose its excitement.

There was the place over the next hill, in the village just up the road, around the next corner. There was never where I was, and there always seemed more promising.

I wish I could do it, Octavio said. Go there.

Leave the bakery, you mean? said Grenelle. Why couldn't you?

Look what happened to Maman. Or Papa.

People leave for a lot of reasons, my boy. Some have no choice. But some just want a bit of adventure, a change from the routine of life. The place I call there is not as cruel as you may think and you don't have to go far to reach it. Sometimes all you need do is walk to the end of the street and turn the corner. And remember, no matter how far you wander, here will always be here.

On the tenth anniversary of the Armistice, the Sunday newspaper contained a collage of hand-tinted photographs framed with banners, flags and crossed rifles: an anniversary commemoration of the bravest generals the war had known. Octavio pointed to a waxed moustache, a cap decorated with laurels, a chest heavy with medals. Monsieur suddenly spoke.

—need to move—been here too long—the snipers have ranged us out. We'll catch one between the eyes if we stay here—need to move—out of the mud—find dry ground. Captain says—keep the sun behind us boys—the Boche—can't see us when they look into the sun—Captain is a fool boys—don't believe a word of it—our friends across the way—can see us—as sure as I see you—perfect silhouettes we make—might as well wear a target on our heads—the Boche don't miss—they never do.

Monsieur struggled to stand, his eyes wide and afraid, sweat beading on his face.

Time to go boys—left right left right—face to the sun—one two one two—let it fall behind you—you're a dead man.

Octavio gave up on the newspapers. They did nothing but frighten his father now. He pulled the *Arabian Nights* from under his bed and blew off a layer of dust.

As Octavio turned page after page to what had been their favourite pictures—the cave of thieves, the sailors in their flying ships, the boy and the golden lamp—his father would only stare. Until Octavio revealed the picture of the princess in her red flowing robes, whispering in the king's ear.

The important thing, Monsieur suddenly said, was that it was red.

———

Madame Lafrouche was paying for her sourdough when she asked after Octavio's father. Octavio told her of his frustration. How the newspapers upset him, how their favourite illustrations in the *Arabian Nights* no longer raised much response. His father was disappearing more and more every day.

You need to leave this place, Madame Lafrouche said. There is too much history, too many memories. Your father needs a change of scenery.

Octavio thought the worst. Glimpses of his father marching away into a summer sun, his mother huddled under a street lamp, the Sisters lifting their lengths of cane flashed in his head as though it had all happened yesterday.

You are a good son, Madame Lafrouche said.

But—where would we go? Octavio said.

Goodness me, nowhere in particular. Just go for a walk, wander around for a while, find some new pictures. You might try the Louvre.

How far is that?

Closer than you think, Madame Lafrouche said.

Blind Grenelle watched as Monsieur clutched at his son's elbow. One foot landed in the street. Octavio stumbled but then caught the balance for both of them. He looked back at Grenelle. The watchmaker smiled.

Remember, he said. A left turn then two streets then turn right. Another two streets then right again. That should get you on your way.

Got it, said Octavio. Left two right two right.

Father and son took another step.

Face to the sun, Monsieur said.

Octavio looked into the sky, then down at his feet. Yes, Papa.

Slowly the Notre-Dame men approached the corner. Grenelle watched them as they vanished.

In the beginning they would make a nervous pair, their strides wary, their pace guarded.

They set out with Grenelle's instructions. Left two right two right, the watch man repeated. That's enough to get you started. He had written the code on the palms of Octavio's hands: *L2* on the left, *R2R* on the right. Octavio remembered the *L* and *R* his mother had marked on the toes of his shoes when he was a boy.

Then you should have no problems, Grenelle had said.

Within weeks the Notre-Dame men had established their own system: a sequence they would follow every Sunday, like a trail of pebbles one could retrace if they ever found themselves lost.

———

There was the barbershop a few streets away. The proprietor had set one of his chairs, an extravagance of wrought iron with levers and handles and gears for raising the seat or adjusting the headrest, on the pavement outside. More often than not a customer was reclined in the chair, laid flat on his back, his face covered in lather, obligingly holding a hand mirror as the barber strapped his razor.

Next to the barbershop: a pedicurist's establishment. A line of men, bored and restless, squirmed on wooden chairs under the shop's window. As Octavio and his father passed the queue, they invariably heard someone ask whose turn it was to go inside and see if their women's nails were dry. The man being shaved would grumble that he would be along in a moment.

Around another corner, if they had kept to their schedule, the Notre-Dames would stop to watch as an old woman, dressed in much finery, stepped from a long black automobile. As her chauffer held the door open, the woman would turn and summon five tiny dogs to follow her in a tangle of leashes into a nearby park. As they waited for the procession to pass, Emile Notre-Dame would name each dog. Henri, Henri, Henri, Henri, Louis, he would say.

Next came the man selling chestnuts, leaning beside a blackened old tin pan, offering his small paper

bags. He wore a tattered beret and a pencil-thin moustache. With one trouser leg folded up and tucked into
his belt, he balanced on a well-worn crutch. There
would be no words exchanged, no formality or cere-
mony, but Octavio's father and the chestnut man
would salute each other as they passed.

And there would be the pigeon woman. In a heavy
winter coat, no matter the weather, she sat on a bench
with a loaf of bread, pulling crumbs and scattering
them to a large crowd cooing patiently at her feet. A
few bolder birds sat on her shoulders, while two or
three others flapped and hovered above her head, waiting for a perch on her head.

Octavio could always count on the woman and her
birds to bring a smile to his father's face.

They were a nervous pair to begin but curiosity would
come to steady their walk. As they wandered Octavio
and his father would peer through shop windows, poke
their heads in mysterious doorways and around blind
corners; stand aside as people rushed about their days.

After a few Sundays they managed to cross the
eighth, arm in arm, hand pressed into hand, the son
steering, the father keeping up as best he could. And
as the weeks and months passed, Octavio could sense
something come over his father, like a series of gentle

tugs on puppet strings, pulling him more upright and strengthening his gait.

At the end of the Champs Élysées the sky opened wide, a great yawn over the Place de la Concorde, as though the city had tired of its tree-lined thoroughfare and needed a good stretch. The square was a blur of traffic. It was all Octavio and his father could do to avoid being run down. Monsieur gripped his son's arm and Octavio remembered his mother's hand squeezing his as they came home from school. Father and son walked on.

Two wheels, four wheels, pushed and pulled and pedalled, grinding brakes, wheezing fumes, yelled obscenities filled their ears. And beyond the square the gardens of the Tuileries beckoned, offering a chair or two in the shade, a chance to catch one's breath after a morning of walking and a minute of braving the mad Concorde whirlwind.

Near the boat pond a groundsman stood on a ladder leaning against the statue of a nymph. The fellow braced himself on the woman's cold stone breast. His other hand held a heavy brush with which he scrubbed the pigeon droppings from her hair. He appeared not to notice the young man pulling two chairs to the edge of the pond.

Octavio checked the position of the sun, adjusted the chairs, and helped his father settle in a comfortable spot. Propping his feet on the water's edge, Octavio closed his eyes, the sun's warmth glowing through his eyelids. A voice shouted behind him.

A fine mess you're making of my gravel, monsieur.

The groundsman was waving his brush. Octavio fell forward and struggled to his feet. His father hunched his shoulders and covered his head with his arms. Octavio looked up and apologized.

We were heading for the museum, monsieur. We just wanted to rest for a moment.

The groundsman grunted and thrust his thumb in the direction of the Louvre, looming through the trees. Put the chairs back when you leave, he said.

The baker stumbles from the cake-slice. His hair juts in clumps from his head; his fingers as curled as hooks. He doubles over, grasping both knees, gulping air still heavy with smoke, fighting the urge to vomit. Drops of sweat fall on his Sunday shoes, raising tiny puffs of ash as they land.

The crowd closes in. Give him some room, the elderly woman barks. For heaven's sake let the poor man breathe.

The old man with the thick spectacles puts an arm around the baker's heaving shoulders, patting him on the back. He murmurs in the man's ear, as though singing a lullaby.

All done now, my boy.

All done now.

Isabeau Normande became a restorer, working as long as daylight glowed through the dingy cellar windows of the Louvre, coaxing grime and neglect from its collections. She had learned her craft at the elbow of one Madame Tessier.

There was no way of guessing how old the woman was, nor in the years Isabeau would spend with her did Madame T show any sign of aging. She arrived at the museum each morning in the same wrinkled state, but from where no one could say.

Naturally there were the myths and legends, hearsay

and lazy notions shared among the custodians. As an infant, like Moses in the reeds, Madame T had been left in a basket on the steps of the museum's grand entrance. That she would outlive them all. That if the woman ever died, she would be interred beneath the armless Venus de Milo or know the reason why.

They met not many days after Isabeau's eighteenth birthday, the spring of 1928, a dark morning of sleet and rain. Isabeau had found her way through the tangle of corridors beneath the museum for her interview. Madame T said nothing as she waved Isabeau to a stool beside her worktable. As Isabeau removed her scarf and adjusted her lock of hair, she noticed a painting spread out on Madame's table.

The woman turned from her work. So mademoiselle, tell me something about your—

Isabeau's nervousness took hold. I see you're working on the *Beggar Boy*, she blurted. Spanish isn't it by Murillo if I remember correctly first name wait don't tell me Bartolomé yes that's it you know I've always been an admirer of his work and this one particularly so dramatic the way he throws the sunlight across the boy and the detail he manages with the basket of fruit why you can almost taste the shrimps and the strange way he poses the boy tells quite a story don't you think when I was little and started coming to the museum I am a devoted visitor you know madame I would spend hours wondering who the boy in the painting was and what was he picking at under his shirt and why were his feet so dirty my goodness I even gave him a name Pedro I think he is such a beautiful boy—

—self, Madame T interrupted.

Isabeau squirmed on her stool. Forgive me, madame. To be sitting *here*, in *this* cellar, is more than I could have imagined. I can get carried away.

So I see, Madame T said. Allow me to explain something, mademoiselle. The problem is that you are much too much in love. You are here because your parents mentioned your name to someone who mentioned your parents' name to someone who mentioned your name to my superior who suggested that I might find a position for you. And so here you sit blocking my light and dripping on my floor, eager to tell me that you love the paintings in my museum. That you have known them, admired them, dreamt of them since you were a little girl. I wish it were otherwise but all this means nothing to me. Everyone who has sat on that stool has claimed your devotion. They have dropped to their knees and confessed that they would do anything, even throw themselves into the Seine, if it would preserve and protect my paintings. As though such foolishness could restore beauty to its rightful place. No, mademoiselle, I need no more suitors here. What I need is a cleaning girl, a scrubber with a vacant head and careful fingers whose fondest wish is to do only as I tell her. On the face of it, you are not that girl. And for that I am sorry.

But I could be that girl, Isabeau said, fighting tears and fumbling with her scarf. Please, madame. A chance is all I ask.

Madame T looked up from a reluctant flake of varnish and slid her magnifying glasses to her forehead. Many a hopeful apprentice had sat before her over the years. She had stared into more portraits than she could count. She could take the measure of someone, in life or in oils, with little more than a glimpse.

She watched Isabeau and waited for that moment, that dullness crossing a young woman's vision and marking her as another daughter of privilege who would not last a week.

It never came. There was something in this one's fidgeting, Madame thought. Certainly not idleness. Perhaps this one was indeed genuine, perhaps the girl did truly love the paintings. Madame T knew they had been her friends all these years, could they not be this girl's as well? Her scowl fell away.

As I said, mademoiselle. On the face of it. But here in the cellars we have an expression: there is always another face.

Madame T lifted Isabeau's chin.

Eyes up. You are in the Louvre, mademoiselle, not the Métro. You will not see anything by looking at your shoes.

Isabeau's uniform was a sad drape of smock with a variety of pliers, tweezers, scrapers, knives and brushes bulging the pockets. On her worktable she had arranged an array of mysterious emulsifiers, each jar and tin neatly aligned with the next. She could turn small wads of cotton across her knuckles—improves the dexterity, Madame T had explained—like a gambler might roll a coin as he considered his next wager.

Removed from the galleries, stripped of their frames and laid flat, the art in Isabeau's care would take on a strange perspective. Hanging on a wall the subject might lock eyes with the visitor and follow them around the salon, but on her table focal points moved elsewhere. Weak chins jutted out, warts and freckles sprang to life; wrinkles and lumps and scars and pocked complexions came to the fore. As though the subjects in the paintings, from the saintly to the common, had found themselves in their physician's office with their pantaloons around their ankles, their socks drooping off the end of the table.

So lay the fourteenth Louis, covered with a film of yellowing gesso and peeling tempera: the accumulations of breath and smoke and stale air stirred by an endless stream of viewers. In defiance of this glaze the Sun King still wore his finest blouse, a lace cravat, silk hosiery; his jowls framed by a mass of black curls. While one hand balanced the royal sceptre the other was tucked against his ample waist, pulling aside his Versailles robes to reveal a pair of dainty red-heeled shoes.

At a nearby table Madame T was bent over a gothic altar screen. How is your man? she said without looking up from her work.

Isabeau hovered in close to Louis' well-turned leg. A few more spots and we will be done, she said.

Not that man, *your* man. Your Sunday fellow. I suppose you'll be wanting to rush up upstairs to see him now?

Isabeau ignored the question.

Frankly, Madame said, I do not quite see the attraction. The way he lurks around the galleries with that crooked old fellow on his arm. Not an ounce of muscle between them. Chattering away at this picture or that. On the face of it I find nothing to recommend him at all.

But on another face? Isabeau said.

You have me there. I admit I have heard the custodians talk. Apparently, some of the more impressionable visitors have taken to swooning.

The woman dipped a swab in a foul-smelling liquid and began wiping a face wailing in the dirt of Calvary. And so to you, my grubby little darling, she said.

A half-circle of schoolgirls fussed with their excursion dresses in an alcove off the Grande Galerie. In front of them hung a riverside scene of modest size. Amid the watercolour's greens and blues of poplars, river grass and calm water a couple could be seen strolling the bank. She wore a yellow dress dappled with sunlight. Her companion lacked any detail; he was merely a dark shape obscured in the shade.

The teacher clapped her hands. The girls ignored her. They were intent on the two men standing in front of the painting. The pair were thin and wiry; their shoulders sloped as each leaned in to examine the watercolour. They wore rumpled suits and scuffed shoes. The young one's hands, folded behind his back, held a soft-brimmed hat. The older one trembled as he gripped his companion's elbow.

The girls' tittering grew louder.

The young man tilted his head to one side and

bounced the hat behind his back. Back and forth went his head, up and down flopped the hat. Every so often he would murmur something. After a moment, the older fellow would respond in kind.

More giggles, spreading now like a fever.

In desperation the teacher pressed a finger to her lips. The resulting silence filled with the voices of the two men: one quiet and deep, with a hint of laughter; the other louder, more abrupt, as though the old fellow were having trouble hearing.

Sweethearts, the young man said.

A duke, said the old one.

And his fiancée—

The famous actress—

Very dramatic.

Strolling along—

Suddenly the skies grow dark.

Looks like rain, he says.

How I hate the rain, she says—

dramatically.

But my darling, says the duke—

do you love me?

The actress turns away.

I do not, monsieur.

But why?

I do not wish to—
to be—
to be—
a duchess!
She pushes him—
in the river and—
and laughs—
and opens her umbrella.
The water—
is only up to the duke's knees—
He flaps his arms—
like he is drowning.
My sweet duke, says the actress.
Of course I love you.
But you pushed me, says the duke.
I was only practising—
says the actress—
my acting,
and you thought—
you were drowning—
silly man.
The duke starts—
laughing.
What is so funny? says the actress.
My darling, says the duke.
It was I who—

who—
was acting!

The young man had mimed along with the tale: a push, a laugh, the flapping arms, another laugh. The school-girls could hardly contain themselves.

The two men turned to find a dozen beaming faces staring up at them. The young man fumbled with his hat, his eyes searching the room as though the alcove had abruptly gone dark. The old man simply grinned. With nowhere to run, the young man extended his arm to one side and bowed deeply.

One of the girls threw her hand in the air.

Monsieurmonsieurmonsieur. Who are they?

The young man was still bent at the waist. Who are who, mademoiselle?

The duke and the actress. Should we give them names?

He looked back at the painting. I suppose we should.

Romeo and Juliet, the girl said.

The young man stroked his chin. Funny names for a duke and an actress, don't you think?

Well they *were* very funny.

As you wish, mademoiselle. The young man straightened, pushed his hat on his head, bowed again to the girls, turned and bowed to the teacher, then took the old man's arm.

———

Isabeau turned away as they brushed past her. She managed a glimpse of the young man's face. She smiled, hoping he might look her way. Remembering herself she adjusted the scarf, a fleeting image of his bright eyes, their corners creased and happy, and his cocked eyebrow still as clear as if he had paused and looked at her. She turned back only to see the two men disappear into the crowded Grande Galerie.

Madame T did not look up from the altar screen.

I do not care to know, Isabeau. It is not my concern what you hope to accomplish or why your man comes here every week or what possesses him to wear the same suit Sunday after Sunday. Do not make excuses about his hat, or retell his stories that have nothing to do with our treasures, or try to explain away his strange companion. I do not want to hear you say words like charming or handsome or clever and please do not say it is because he loves the paintings because I have heard that one before.

If you must know, madame, it is his eyes, Isabeau said.

Let me guess. Pools of mystery?

The brightest grey, madame.

The brigade retreats from the rooftop. The baker seems to look in the young woman's direction, his unseeing eyes, like those of a trapped animal, sending a shiver through her. She turns away, hunching her shoulders and shrinking herself, willing his dark stare to glance off. The cold damp of being noticed, called out and pointed at, spreads down her back.

The baker looks away and shuffles through the crowd. The young woman hears a few hushed voices.

If there is anything we can do, monsieur.

Anything at all. You need only ask.

I can lend you a few books, monsieur.

If it would help you start again.

The woman hides in the crowd, moving as far from the baker as she can. She squeezes herself against the bakery's windows.

The firemen emerge from the cake-slice, wiping their faces and lighting their cigarettes. The captain barks and they merge again into one creature, rolling its hoses, storing its equipment, leaving its sooty footprints unattended.

The snow begins to ease.

Her work would begin before sunrise; the painstaking search for cracks to be filled, dust to be uprooted, flakes of colour to be returned. Her back ached, hunched over her table for hours at a stretch. Her eyes stung, unable to blink for fear of missing something in the poor early light of the cellars.

Isabeau Normande would take her lunch by the boat pond. A few slices of apple, a bite of sausage, a small wedge of cheese; a book, a chair, and a blissfully straightened backbone.

She would select a chair from under the trees and

pull it to a habitual spot. Noting the height of the sun, she would push its legs into the gravel and settle herself. If the day were warm she might remove her shoes, roll off her stockings and dip a foot in the water, giving her toes a painful stretch. Then she would begin reading, ignoring the children launching their toy boats as they puffed their cheeks to fill the sails.

A few pages along and something would cause her to rummage for a pencil. She would then underline with deliberate strokes, write exclamation points in the margins. In other books on other days she might circle whole paragraphs, marking them with a flurry of question marks. She folded corners, filled gutters with strips of paper, drew giant Xs through page after page, or traced a box around a phrase or opinion and connected it with a wandering line to another box she had drawn at the bottom of the page. There, in a determined hand, she would write down her own thinking on the matter.

Absorbed in such conversation, Isabeau might forget about eating altogether. It could be days later when Madame T would sit up from her own table, look over at Isabeau and ask if anyone had noticed the smell of rotting fruit.

On those warm days the Pont des Arts seemed to be the centre of the city. The latest fashions strolled across and back—one could mark the seasons, the years, by the length of uncovered legs, the width of hips, the reveal of cleavage. Lovers with timid natures or brazen embraces draped themselves along the railings. Picnickers unrolled their blankets, shared their confits and poured their wines. Protesters marched shoulder to shoulder with banners demanding justice or anarchy, more wages or less work. Only the view from the bridge, together with the number of dogs, remained unchanged.

For Jacob Kalb, the picnickers would leave too many remains of their luncheons to blow and scatter underfoot. The protesters would break ranks and run amok, scattering the dogs that would then threaten to upend his easel. The fashionables would offer too many opinions as they stood peering over his shoulder.

Wishing for a good rain to dampen the crowds, Jacob would pack his carpetbag and move along to the Tuileries. There he would draw portraits for those willing to stop moving back and forth and just sit quietly, or perhaps spend a coin or two on something to hang in the parlour.

He came to recognize the garden's habitual visitors. The card sharps, a pair of old men who arrived on Thursday mornings to play a hand or two of *belote* under the statue of Diana. The one who calmly worked his pipe always held the winning deal, the one with the dangling unlit cigarette then cursing the heavens and throwing his cards at his opponent. Tuesdays brought forth the knitters: sitting with their backs to each other, gossiping about their menfolk like women half as young, turning out hand after hand of thick red mittens. And on Sundays the reader: a young woman sitting alone by the boat pond. Jacob would watch as she selected a chair from under the nearby trees, dragged it to the same spot and propped her feet at the pond's edge. Her face always hidden by a lock of hair; always buried in a book.

Jacob had decided the young woman was a native of the city. She seemed unconcerned with what was going on around her, and he had been turned away by enough aloofness to know better than to ask. He would continue strolling the gardens, searching for someone else's money to pay for a new page in his sketching book or a bowl of soup for his belly.

But for one day. As he turned his back on the young woman and began heading in the direction of the trees, Jacob Kalb remembered something the Barbarian had said. Long before, in those first good days at the Academy.

They were practising the rendering of drapery: folds, highlights and shadow, weightless volumes, suggestions of form beneath the peaks and hollows of fabric. Jacob sat with a small drawing table covered by a few sheaves of paper balanced across his knees. At the front of the room a model reclined on a chaise, the man's thick body covered in swaths of brocade. He lay with his flabby arms behind his head, his eyes half closed and roaming the ceiling in boredom. The drawing master sat in a corner, timing the students with a pocket watch.

Jacob worked, erased, and reworked a series of creases where the brocade fell away from the mound of a large stomach. Next to him sat another student, the one everyone called the Barbarian.

Your work is good, mi amigo. Though I think you might be trying too hard.

Something isn't right, Jacob said. I can't seem to find it.

Perhaps that something is not you. Perhaps it is what you are trying to draw.

Jacob peeked at the Barbarian's table. The sheet of paper was blank.

What are you waiting for? Jacob said.

Something interesting, mi amigo. The Barbarian put aside his table and approached the model.

In your place, monsieur, the master said. The Barbarian whispered in the model's ear, then took one of the man's arms from behind his head and draped it across his eyes.

Monsieur!

The Barbarian thanked the model, returned to his chair and began to draw. Jacob watched as the beginnings of a face quickly emerged. Not a fold or crease of brocade appeared on the paper.

We are supposed to be practising drapery, Jacob said.

That I can see, said the Barbarian.

Jacob introduced himself. You are the first person to ever say my work is good.

It is certainly better than our master's over there, Jacob. And it is certainly better than mine. The name is Carlos.

I thought you were el Bárbaro, Jacob said.

For the masters I am the Barbarian. For you I am simply Carlos, trying to be an artist like you.

You still haven't drawn any fabric.

But what you cannot see is more interesting, do you not think? For me what is hidden, like our model's face, is the swirl of cape to a bull.

A bull?

Or a barbarian, if you will.

Jacob cleared his throat. A portrait, mademoiselle?

Isabeau checked the lock of hair hanging across her cheek. She did not look up.

I don't think so, monsieur.

I could use the practice, Jacob said.

I am sorry, no. Thank you.

From afar, mademoiselle. I will keep my distance, there, under the trees. I can sketch you as you read. You won't be disturbed.

Isabeau looked up. Her hair moved from her face to reveal a hint of profile, a glimpse of a scar. No, she said.

Jacob had not eaten in days. He couldn't waste the midday light touting something that would not sell, but his stomach pushed him on.

It will take so little of your time, mademoiselle.

Isabeau's face was set in anger, fighting back tears.

Jacob shrugged. And cost you almost nothing.

Isabeau lowered her book to her lap as Jacob turned to leave. She looked at Jacob's clothes, the rags hanging off his shoulders, the frayed cuffs of his trousers. Again she touched the lock of her hair. After a moment, she wiped her eyes and called after him.

Very well, monsieur. On condition.

Jacob suggested she might lower her chin. Your cheek will hide in the shadow, mademoiselle. I assure you. It is a very alluring pose.

Isabeau shifted in the chair and lowered her head. Her hair fell in a soft curve. Jacob held up his hand.

There. Please hold still.

One eye looked back at him.

He began a simple oval, leaning to one side. Then a midline. And a line for the eyes, one for the mouth, another for the nose. Jacob sharpened her jaw, hollowed the visible cheek. One side of the oval he left blank. He would fill the shadow later.

A fine start, mademoiselle.

Isabeau's visible eye next. Dark and set deep in the socket: returning the viewer's stare and glistening.

As he worked Jacob asked if she was enjoying her book.

I am not, Isabeau said. It is trying very hard to explain the Cubists.

Theirs is a different approach, mademoiselle.

Isabeau lifted her face. A difficult one, you mean.

Head down please. Difficult?

Distorted, said Isabeau. Unrecognizable, undisciplined. Like the work of an amateur.

I see, mademoiselle. Should art be recognizable?

It should resemble something.

What does your book think?

Isabeau fanned the pages and stopped at a painting. She showed the page to Jacob. He studied the image and returned to his work. Isabeau read aloud.

Consider Portrait of Love. *Here the viewer is presented*

with an enormous head, we can assume a female's, bursting with angles, thrusts and textures.

A fair definition of the movement, mademoiselle. Though perhaps somewhat vague. Does your book mention how the Cubists use their colour?

Isabeau continued reading. *The raw oranges and reds and greens prove an eloquent simile for the ceremonial masks and warrior shields of tribal—*

They do love the primitive, Jacob said.

—Africa, rendered as simple planes and geometric shapes, bordered in thick black line, composed to offer an incisive portrait of a three-dimensional object within the confining flatness of paint and canvas.

Jacob smiled. There it is, mademoiselle. We are meant to see everything at once. The Cubists are known for hiding nothing. Putting on display everything that can be seen, and more importantly, that cannot be seen. Emotional beauty is what they are after, in all its perspectives.

But I see no beauty here, Isabeau said.

The title may offer a clue, Jacob said.

Portrait of Love?

Jacob stopped drawing. Think of the artist, mademoiselle.

I suppose he has painted his lover.

Why not his passion?

How can we see another's emotion?

We can imagine it, Jacob said. Picture the artist standing at his easel, consumed by the woman sitting before him. He loses control. He cannot get the colours off his brush fast enough. He paints, you might say, like an amateur. He pays no attention to anatomy, to perspective, to scale. What appears on the canvas is unrecognizable to us. But to him it is what is in his head, in his heart, in his belly.

But wouldn't his inspiration be her physical beauty? Isabeau said. Why not paint that? Why not render it truthfully, down to the finest detail?

Who is to say he did not, mademoiselle?

No one wants to look at ugliness.

Is it so ugly, so amateurish as you say, or simply a passionate view? Consider a stained glass window, mademoiselle. It is crafted by a man who knows nothing about art. Moreover he has never witnessed a miracle, no angel has ever appeared above his bed, he wouldn't recognize God if he passed Him on the street. And yet faith fills his heart. That thing he cannot see, that passion, fires his imagination and guides his glass cutter.

And I suppose we look up from our pews and see heaven, Isabeau said.

Or the recognizable, mademoiselle.

———

Jacob brushed away bits of eraser. He moved to turn his sketchbook around and reveal his work. Isabeau raised her hand and looked away. Thank you for the conversation, she said.

She handed him a few coins. Please keep the sketch, monsieur. I know what I look like.

The crowd reluctantly begins to melt away.

The poor man will have to sleep in the cellar, someone says.

At least the bakery wasn't harmed, someone replies. We will still have our breads.

His father did his share of sleeping in the cellar, after the war and all.

The apple doesn't fall far.

He is a strong one, our man. He'll be back at the ovens in no time.

The holiday will cheer him up.

It will cheer us all up.

By mid-week the neighbourhood women will be dancing belly to belly, a Savoy swing being the rage of the
summer. Their men will toast their bicycle gods and
their cabaret lovelies and sing themselves hoarse. Their
children will perform handstands and balancing tricks,
pull monster faces and roller skate through the dancers.

In the evening the garlands of flags will droop to the
street, the light bulbs flickering on to burn themselves
out in all the excitement. Below the dripping ruins of the
cake-slice there will be more dancing, more dreams of
breaking from the peloton in the last fifty metres to win
the Tour, more imaginings of tempting hips and firm
breasts, each curve and nipple revealed on the stage
through soft feathers and small Japanese fans.

The old man with the thick spectacles might find
the baker sitting in front of the Boulangerie Notre-
Dame, watching the celebrations. They might share a
glass of wine, or talk of rebuilding a library. The baker's
foot might unconsciously keep time with the music.

If fortune is kind to this corner of the eighth, such
will be their holiday. Bastille Day, 1938.

Jacob opened his sketching book.

A man with a meticulous goatee, wearing the overalls of a factory worker from the *banlieue*, captured in mid-stride as he pulls on a leash. His pet—a rabbit fat enough for the pot, ears dragging on the ground, legs digging in—resists at the other end as the pair take a turn under the trees. In the drawing the detail is minuscule: a steady hand at work. One could have plucked individual hairs from the reluctant animal's tail.

A woman in clumsy makeup leans against a lantern post, playing something on her accordion. A well-dressed man, arms and legs frozen in a dancer's pose, bows to drop a coin in the cup at her feet. At a glance one might think his limbs had been dislocated. A closer look reveals a graceful line from shoulder to fingertip, as if he once might have stood in a spotlight, shading his eyes in search of the balconies, the audience calling for one more progression across the stage.

On a bench a girl wears a crown of spring flowers. She sits wrapping bunches of twigs with lengths of ribbon. The baskets around her are filled with lavender. The handwritten sign hanging from her neck suggests *a fragrant bouquet makes a welcoming home.* The curl of the ribbons will need more definition in the final drawing.

A black man, his pomaded grey hair sharply parted, wears the threadbare remains of a tuxedo. He sits in a child's chair with a plank across his knees, the rough wood painted to resemble piano keys. The drawing has frozen the moment as the fellow raises his long fingers above the board, waiting for the conductor's baton, ready to flourish a dramatic opening scale through the low notes.

Three Oriental gentlemen in three top hats and three morning suits, with three boutonnières in three lapels, confer near the garden's ornate entry gates. Two of them wave their walking sticks in opposite directions; the third consults a map. A generous handling of heavy pencil, together with strokes of eraser, renders the silk hatbands with such realism that the drawing could pass for a photograph.

A boy in short trousers, polished boots and straw hat is perched on the edge of the boat pond. He cradles a sailboat in his arms, the vessel in full sail, as long as he is tall. The mainmast tricolour flutters in an unseen breeze. The boy peeks at the viewer from under his master's cap. His eyes are sure, his grin proud, his freckles abundant.

A Tuileries groundsman rests against the plinth of a statue lighting his afternoon smoke. His rake leans beside him. Theseus and the Minotaur are an exacting pencil study of straining muscle and certain death. They ignore the groundsman and the cloud of smoke around his head as they grapple on their perch above him.

Jacob Kalb closed his book, the dream taste of a rabbit stew lingering in his mouth. Another week's work. There were no buyers.

Thick fog settled along the river. Those passing the bookstalls, chins tucked into collars, were hurrying somewhere else.

Somewhere warm and dry, Henri Fournier thought. He shifted on his stool, pulled his father's coat around his shoulders and looked up and down the quay. He lifted his grandfather's book from the stall.

Vague and lost, Henri.

Henri laid the book on the pavement.

Left on the verso. Right on the recto.

And placed a foot on each page.

Gently, Henri. As weightless as feathers now.

Henri pushed his sleeves to his elbows, spread his arms, raised his face to the sky and closed his eyes.

He saw himself walking on eggs, curling his toes over the cool white shells. The eggs dissolved into sand. He was at the edge of the sea, the waves eroding the beach under his feet, sinking them into the warm muck. Another wave slipped up the shore and circled his ankles. He heard the rasp of a voice. Excuse me, it said. He looked down to watch the ooze slide away, loosen its grip, ready to release him into the air. The voice coughed.

Excuse me, monsieur.

Henri opened an eye. Dark bloodshot eyes sunk in wrinkled sockets stared back at him.

Yes? Henri said.

My apologies, monsieur.

It came to Henri. You're the painter, aren't you? From the bridge.

Jacob extended a quivering hand. The name is Kalb, he said. And yes, the bridge has been home for a while now.

There are worse places, I suppose, Henri said. Can I interest you in something? My stock is a little out of date I'm sorry to say, but I think I could recommend a title or two.

I am somewhat short of funds at the moment, Jacob said. Actually, I thought I might sell you something.

But that is *my* job, Monsieur Kalb. Selling, you see.

And how is business? Jacob said, attempting a smile.

Henri raised an eyebrow. It could be better. And yours? The art goes well, does it?

I mostly do portraits. For people in the Tuileries. I manage a few coins now and then.

Henri thought he could smell something foul. He scanned Jacob's clothes. I see, he said.

But lately I've been doing work for my own pleasure, Jacob said. To break the monotony of all those faces, you understand.

Perfectly, Henri said. He knew a lie when he heard one. He imagined there hadn't been a face willing to sit in some time.

I was wondering if you might be interested in selling them, Jacob said.

Alas, monsieur, I am not in the art business.

The ladies on your postcards might say otherwise, monsieur—?

Fournier. Booksellers since the dawn of time.

Jacob began rummaging through the bag at his feet. Henri knew what was coming. He was embarrassed for the man, but didn't want to offend.

Monsieur Kalb, please.

Call me Jacob.

Monsieur Kalb, I am a humble bookseller. Once in a very long while, yes, I manage to sell a postcard.

If you don't think my work has merit, Monsieur Fournier—

Henri, please.

—I can move along and try another stall. But I doubt I would find one painted such a remarkable shade of green.

The others will rob you blind, Henri said.

Then I am in the right place, Jacob said.

Henri hesitated. Very well. One look.

Jacob pulled his sketchbook from the bag. He removed the drawing of the boy with the sailboat.

An honest opinion is all I ask, he said.

Henri held it at arm's length, wondering whether such an opinion would involve turning one's head or stroking one's chin or both.

Every day he could see the Louvre from his stool. Yet the thought of locking up the stall for an afternoon, of actually visiting the museum, had never occurred to him. He was a sole proprietor of a book-stall; there was no time for anything else. He knew nothing of art, good or bad. What he knew was life on the quay: selling books to people who did not want them, watching homeless souls emerge every day from under the Pont des Arts, wishing he had not been born a Fournier.

Jacob proposed an arrangement. They would split the earnings. If his work was still hanging in the book-stall after a month, he would put it back in his sketch-ing book and move on.

Henri examined the detail in the drawing. There was a twinkle, rendered with a tiny spot of white, in the little sailor's eye. He shook Jacob's hand.

We have a deal, my friend. One month. What do you call this piece?

The boy claimed he was an admiral, Jacob said.

The partners—Jacob at his spot on the bridge, Henri on his stool—would acknowledge each other with a distant wave, a shrug and a better-luck-tomorrow shake of the head. The Admiral managed to stop a few passersby but no one dug into their pockets or fumbled through their purses.

One day, after weeks of grey skies, the bridge became almost impassable with people enjoying some sun and warmth. Henri watched as Jacob packed his easel and carpetbag and headed in the direction of the Tuileries.

As Henri locked up the stall that evening, he realized that Jacob had not returned.

Days passed without any sign of the painter.

Henri's eyes drooped shut, his head flopped to one side. He caught himself falling off the stool. As he found his balance Jacob was standing in front of him, a sheet of paper rolled under his arm.

I was beginning to think you had found another bridge, Henri said. Where have you been?

Jacob looked up and down the quay as though he had awoken from a nightmare and did not know where he was.

Working, he said. He handed Henri the paper. I've been working—trying—to eat.

Henri had never seen someone so pale and withered. He thought his friend's voice had changed. There was a stumble, a stutter. He realized Jacob was having trouble finding the words.

You *have* been busy, Henri said.

He held the paper at arm's length. It was the face of a young woman, shadowed by a curve of hair, one visible eye looking back at the bookseller.

She looks familiar, Henri said, popping his head above the drawing. Have I seen her before?

—a customer—yours? Jacob mumbled.

I don't think so, said Henri. Now wait a moment. I know where.

Henri handed the portrait back to Jacob and began running his hand along the row of books in the stall.

Here it is, he said, pulling out a book of ancient myths. He flipped back and forth through the pages. Yes, I was right. You see here? Fortuna, the goddess of luck.

Jacob looked at the book, then at his drawing. He wavered on his feet, catching himself against the stall.

When did you last eat? Henri said.

Henri tacked Fortuna beside the Admiral, taking care to smooth the corners of her paper. He reached into the stall, removed a metal box, handed Jacob a few francs.

An advance, my friend.

The crowd is gone. The young woman stands alone in front of the dark windows of the bakery.

Through her reflection she sees at first only shapes and outlines: a display case, a monstrous cash register, empty wicker baskets. She cups her hands to her face, pressing her nose against the glass. As her eyes adjust to the dimness within, she pictures how the bakery might once have appeared. The buxom woman with her armload of wheat, the cherubim and their trays of pains au chocolat, the laughing baker, all would be looking down on a morning of jostling customers. The aromas would be something she could only dream.

The street is still now, empty but for the scattering of ashes, yet the young woman senses something else. As if she had walked into a darkened room, could hear the sound of breathing. She cannot bring herself to turn around.

That it would come was inevitable, yet for Emile Notre-Dame it would take its own time. Death would not arrive quick and merciful. It would be his memories that would take their invisible toll. What he had felt: the wet and cold of the mud pulling him back into the trench, the stumble, the fall into blind terror as he managed to finally crawl out and run. What he had seen: his friends running in the other direction, into the metal hail pouring from the sky, running until the ground swallowed them up. What he had heard: their agonies fading as he disappeared into the dawn mist.

———

Their Sunday walks continued. All weathers, all seasons. Emile and Octavio's outings became a habit for the entire neighbourhood, as ordinary as dawn breaking in the east. So ordinary that when Mondays arrived, customers had stopped asking if father and son had seen anything new at the Louvre the day before or if they were offering a new story this morning.

And no one save for Blind Grenelle and Madame Lafrouche noticed as Emile began to fade away altogether, his face a deepening hollow, his once agile fingers curling into awkward fists.

In those last weeks the watchmaker wanted to remind Octavio that he was his own man, that his father had taught him well. Madame Lafrouche wished she could find a way to tell him that his father's stories would carry on. But both of them sensed that Octavio did not want to hear such things. He wanted still to be his father's son.

The walks grew shorter and all but ended. The Sunday stories dwindled to a few scattered words, then stopped altogether.

One evening after locking up, Octavio found his father lying on the table in the cellar, his hands at last unclenched and resting on his chest.

With the ovens ticking in the darkness, Octavio sat through the night, watching over the Thinnest Baker in All Paris. He imagined the marble table making one more journey. His father would have loved a return ride across a sea teeming with sharks and mermaids, and a wife standing in a Tuscan quarry to greet him with raspberry tarts, a treat after such a long journey.

With the first hints of sunrise, Octavio turned the sign in the window of the bakery. WE ARE SORRY TO BE CLOSED. PLEASE CALL AGAIN.

To the gravediggers, it looked as though half the eighth was standing at the graveside when they lowered Emile into the ground.

Grenelle opened the family bible. Squinting behind his spectacles, in a clumsy Italian he read a passage about casting one's bread upon the waters. Amid the circle of mourners one of the gravediggers mumbled to himself. Are we sure the fellow is in there, he said. I've planted heavier coffins in my time.

When the service ended Grenelle invited everyone to return to the bakery. To dry our eyes, he said, and raise a glass to the man who made our breakfasts all those years. Octavio said he would be along soon. As it began to rain, Octavio took shelter under a large plane tree, green with the buds of spring leaves.

He remembered walking with his father. He stepped back into the rain, straightened the flowers on the grave's mound of freshly dug earth and turned in the direction of the trees of the Tuileries.

Walking along the garden's promenade overlooking the river, Octavio heard a gravelled voice behind him.

The name's Le Drop, monsieur.

The small man perched on a child's stool. He wore the remains of a tuxedo, the ends of his trouser legs trailing bits of thread and bunching around his shoes. Long fingers peeked from the sleeves of his jacket. A plank painted with piano keys was balanced across his knees. He bowed his head and with a quivering hand touched the brim of an invisible cap.

Requests taken and requests played, monsieur. Toe-tapping tunes and tales of wonder, yours for the asking.

Le Drop gathered his sleeves around his elbows, locked his hands together and stretched his arms in front of him. He danced his fingers from one end of the painted keys to the other. As his hands leaped off the end of the plank, Octavio noticed their tremors had disappeared. Play your best, he said.

I happen to know just such a tune, Le Drop said. He started with a double chord, his thumbs stretched long and thin, straining for the octaves. He talked as he played.

Came over in '18 I did, one of the Harlem boys. Hellfighters they called us, keen as flip knives. Keen to do our bit, maybe dance with old Fritz a step or two. But the generals said music was our bit. Shipped us over as an orchestra, yours truly handling the accordion duties. So we arrive in your fair city and march up and down the Champs, looking sharp, playing tight. Tight as new shoes. Ceremonials, hymns, the ragtime when the sweat was up. Folks loved us jazzy joes. But it was the white boys doing all the fighting and we wanted in. Get us up front, we said, take us to the dance. So the generals said well if you've got the itch then we will surely scratch it. And they sent us off to the sharp end. You'll tango with old Fritz now, they said.

Le Drop paused, lingering in the middle keys.

I guess you were too young, boy, for all that fuss.

Octavio nodded. But my father fought. He never talked about it though.

No surprise there, Le Drop said as his fingers wandered through the high notes. Not much to recommend it. Mile after scummy mile it was, all stumps and mud and bones. But we were ready to give old Fritz some of his own. Ready like when you're on the dance floor, one hand cradling your honey's soft soft fingers, your other hand looping round that silky silky waist.

And she's got that look and you've practised the steps a hundred times. Your toes are tapping like they're burning inside your boots. You wait on that downbeat, praying your honey is a real twirler. Then the sergeant puffs his cheeks. You cock your heel and squeeze those fingers. He blows that damn whistle and you're over the top. All the while your honey's spinning like one of those dervishes and you hold on to that waist for dear life. That was how ready we were.

A right-handed progression, soft touches through the black keys, one foot nudging invisible pedals.

I'll wager he was a dancer, your father. Gave your mother a turn no doubt, back in the day. We soldiers knew how to treat the mademoiselles.

Octavio pictured his parents waltzing at a street party, patriotic banners strung above their heads. The figures were fleeting, the flags out of focus. He rubbed at his eyes.

What was it like? he said. Your war.

Le Drop leaned in close to the keyboard. A bit different from your father's, if he was lucky. We dug a lot of trench. Slopping rats and freezing water. Hard labour it was. Coloured labour. Doing our bit, the generals said. So one morning we were shovelling and old Fritz started throwing shells our way. Maybe he was aiming at someone else but with the ground torn up and the front zigging and the wire zagging and the vermin and the dead bodies and all, well old Fritz's aim became a slippery thing. But he just kept on throwing. Screamed those shells did, flying through the air like cats pushed off a ledge.

Le Drop's wrists crossed, hand over hand, climbing through the middle keys. Tears ran down Octavio's face. He saw his father crouched in the cellar of a bombed-out building, mice scurrying over mouldy loaves of bread. Le Drop played on.

Now I'd rather be called a dumb-ass ape than be pruned at the shoulders Hun style, so when those cats started screaming I dropped in six-eight time and buried my face in the slop. Sergeant said it was the funniest thing he had ever seen. Called me the Chocolate Drop. Hey Drop, he'd say, you hear that cat? Just to see me jump. I didn't hear anything but came up with a mouthful all the same. He was most annoying, the sergeant was. From Baton Rouge as I recall. Played everything in a minor key, mournful stuff. Last I saw of him his horn and him were heading home. But he left a little something behind for old Fritz. I couldn't say what the loss of that arm did to his playing. Not much I suppose. Like I said, we were tight. Tight as new shoes.

His fingers splayed wide, Le Drop landed the heavy chords.

My father had a nickname, Octavio said. People used to call him the Thinnest Baker in All Paris.

A fine name hard earned no doubt, Le Drop said, then carried on.

The shells were persistent but I managed to keep all my pieces nonetheless. The gas though, that was something else. There's no hole deep enough to get Le Drop out from under that creeping yellow shit, if you'll pardon the expression. So I came back with these weepy eyes. Now there isn't much call for a keyboard boy who can't read the sheets but this city knows how to treat someone of my particular shade. So when old Fritz finally went home I planted some roots right where you see me. Been here most every day since. Requests taken and requests played.

Le Drop held a final note, one finger deep in the low keys.

He came home, Octavio said.

Le Drop smiled. Like I said, one lucky fellow. What was his proper name?

Octavio choked as he said it.

It's good to remember the real man, Le Drop said. Mine is Walker in case you were wondering. Abraham L Walker, at your service. Mother named me for the great emancipator but she and Mr Lincoln are long passed so I doubt they'd notice the change. She would have liked it though. That's a fine one, she'd say. My boy Le Drop. A fine name hard earned.

They sat watching the river traffic, trading stories about joints and dives and grand halls with floors like polished glass, rooms that could have held a thousand people.

Jittering, Le Drop said. Like everyone was dancing on one set of legs.

About how much butter to turn into the croissant dough.

Enough to make your mouth water just to think of them, Octavio said. And to fill your belly for a week.

About cabaret women and Japanese fans.

So beautiful those girls actually glowed, Le Drop said. I swear you had to shade your eyes.

About the perfect baguette.

You need to tap it, Octavio said. The side of your thumb against the bottom of the loaf. My father called it bakery music.

Your father sounds like a fine fellow, Le Drop said.

I miss his stories, Octavio said.

No doubt there was a nice melody about him.

He loved his newspaper. Every Sunday. We would look at the pictures. When I got older we would visit the museum.

Music and pictures, Le Drop said. Don't they just go together, bring out the finest in people. You two ever read anything or was all this storytelling just made up from pictures? My eyes may not be what they once were, but there was a time when I read every chance I could find. Back in Harlem if you wanted a good tune you needed a good story.

I have a book, Octavio said.

Just one? You're sure one is enough? Young man, you strike me as the sort of fellow who could put a whole shelf to good use.

Octavio stepped onto the Pont des Arts. The rain had stopped. But for the crowds he could have noticed a painter working at his easel near the middle of the bridge. He could have stopped and stood behind the artist, keeping a discreet distance, crossing his hands in the small of his back as he considered the canvas on the easel. He could have thought of his father and whispered a word or two to begin their game.

Instead, he pushed on through the crowds to the end of the bridge and turned in the direction of the booksellers.

At the rear of the bakery above the cellar door, a pencil portrait hangs in a simple frame. The drawing reminds the young woman of the Old Masters: her Dürer, her David, a touch of her Ingres. She recognizes the balance of light and dark, one side alive with contour, the other shrouded in heavy shading; the lift of one corner of the mouth, the sharp glint in the one eye looking back at the viewer; the graceful line of white through the hair.

Suddenly the feeling that she is not alone in the street disappears. She holds her breath, covers her mouth. She knows the face in the portrait.

The war's histories remained in the Fournier stall long after its battles had ended. Among the newspapers clipped to the front of the stall, a few dated back to black days now twenty years gone.

One featured an illustration of a solitary grave in a country field. In the distance a stand of trees waved barren amputated limbs. A few sheep nibbled at shoots of new grass and wildflowers surrounding the smooth mound of earth. The sun was bright and high in the illustration, the sky a pale and peaceful blue. The grave was marked: a tiny tricolour curled lazily while a white cross, made from hand-split pickets and tilting to one side, rose out of the mound. A wreath of poppy blooms hung from the cross. Strands of rusted barbed wire, stretched between four curled iron posts, protected the grave. In the sky above the sheep an ornate banner of words hovered.

Wearing a heavy overcoat Henri Fournier hunched on his stool, turned the front page, and read the old newspaper's headlines. Every few minutes he would push his spectacles against his nose. He did not notice the man standing nearby, dressed in a suit too big for his thin frame, his hands nervously working the brim of a hat.

VICTORY! OUR HEROES RETURNED!

It was the word the telegram had used. Corporal Mabillon had not been wounded, he had not been killed; he was neither heroic nor returned. He had been *lost*. The war department might as well have said Henri's best friend had wandered off like a dreamy schoolboy; that someone was out looking for him at that very moment. That if the corporal had been clever enough to lie his way to the front, then he was wiser still for the adventure and could now lie his way home.

NATURE'S FINAL BLOW!

As the war ended, the Spanish fever had taken its turn. Other friends disappeared in ways even the army could not have dreamed of.

No, the doctor had told Henri, we cannot blame the influenza. Your grandfather and father have been lost to the river. Two lifetimes spent standing in the damp of the quays and the creeping cold finally made its way into their lungs.

Lost. Henri remembered the gape of the doctor's mouth as he said the word.

Henri's mother never again visited the bookstall. She cursed her only son, certain the evil green box on the quay would be his coffin, and not for one minute longer would she stay to watch his own suicide. She had moved to the south to live with an aunt. As she stepped onto the train, Henri had told her his grandfather would not have abandoned the books.

Henri shook his head. The old man couldn't leave the books, he muttered. He began to laugh.

Visions drifted in and out. A cart piled high, drowned cats, Mabillon landing a mouthful on the head of a passing barge captain. Dreams and plans and hopes replaced by a damp life on the quay. Henri imagined himself gathering armloads from the stall, throwing everything into the river, jumping in after. He saw his body floating under the Pont des Arts, lying on a blanket of news-papers and postcards and books.

His laughter became a fit. His spectacles hazed over, his eyes stung, his chest began to ache. A couple passing by stared at the bookseller then hurried on their way, bumping past the man still standing near the stall. Henri rubbed his eyes and wrapped his father's coat tighter around himself.

I remember that newspaper, said the man with the hat.

Henri looked up.

From when I was a boy, the man continued. My father told me it was a noble thing. Putting the grave of such an honourable man on the front of a newspaper.

Henri closed the newspaper. An honourable man?

The man nodded. Very noble, monsieur. All of France in mourning. Even his sheep have gathered to pay respects.

Henri read the banner floating above the grave: REST WELL OUR BRAVE WARRIORS! Your father was a wise man, he said.

The man did not seem to hear. He was staring at the portraits hanging in the stall: the boy and his boat, and the woman veiled in shadow. The hat flopped up and down behind his back as he leaned in for a closer look.

Octavio fumbled through his pockets. He pulled out a handful of centimes, a few crumpled notes. Looking back and forth between the woman and the money in his hand, he counted over and over and over again.

Henri watched the rattle of loose coins. He waited for a decision, doubting the man would buy more than a postcard. A nervous customer rarely committed to anything other than naked flesh; at best one might choose a thin volume in poor condition and then complain about the price. Yet there was something different in this one. Henri noticed how the man's eyes darted in every direction only to return to the woman in the drawing. This one was not interested in a bargain.

May I be of assistance, monsieur? Henri said.

Octavio closed his eyes. He pictured his father standing beside him, stroking his chin and pondering his selections. Which ones would his father choose? There weren't any pictures; apart from their colour each book looked the same. Would he have picked by size then? Would he walk back and forth in front of the stall, pulling a few volumes, weighing them in his hands, calculating how much he could carry back to the cake-slice? Octavio imagined his father whispering so the bookseller would not hear.

Red, the thinnest baker might say. The colour of passion, my boy, of beating hearts and action. They're the bold ones, the reds, sure to be full of adventure. Or we could pick the blue ones, like the wide sea and those mermaids singing us home. Or perhaps the green of the trees in our Tuileries.

Octavio knew his father would assign each colour he saw. The golds would contain tales of treasure hunters and lost cities, the purples would conjur magic and spirits and fairy worlds. He wondered if his father would have considered black a colour at all. Regardless, he would have started with the red ones.

Octavio scanned the books in the stall. There were so many shades of red. Light cloths, bright leathers, blood edges. He listened for his father's voice again.

Imagine a woman, my boy. Watch her as she steps out of a pastry shop. She does not look your way but, oh yes, you see her. Her face, her mouth, the curve of those red lips. You cannot resist. You wonder what would it be like to kiss those lips. As red as raspberries. You bump against her and find yourself sitting in the gutter. The red of raspberries, my boy. That is the colour we'll start with.

Octavio opened his eyes and looked to the portrait of the woman. He watched her mouth. He imagined the tip of her tongue sliding out to wet them. He felt himself leaning in and tilting his head. Closing his eyes as her mouth drew near to his.

Octavio stumbled back from the stall. I—would like a book.

Then monsieur, Henri said, you have come to the right place. I happen to have a few.

Octavio dropped his money, the coins scattered. A red one, if you please.

He quickly pointed at a narrow spine in the first row.

The Plato, Henri said.

Octavio surveyed the spines and pointed again.

Flaubert, monsieur. A very eclectic choice.

Near the end of the stall, a spine wrapped in wine-coloured linen jutted above its neighbours. Octavio pulled the book, a treatise on hydraulics, and handed it to Henri. The bookseller raised an eyebrow.

Quite a lot of reading here, monsieur. You might prefer something, shall we say, more imaginative. Henri selected a book of poetry, bound in a textured black leather.

Octavio shook his head. No, thank you. The red will do for now.

Henri located a ball of twine at the back of the stall and began tying the three books together. As you wish, monsieur.

Octavio looked into the sky. The sun had moved to the west. His father murmured in his ear. Make room for the birds, my boy.

Heading home through the Tuileries, Octavio organized in his head. The reds would be first, light to dark, golds to oranges to rusts. The blues next, then the purples, the greens, the yellows. A library in the cake-slice apartment filled his mind. Books were everywhere: lining the walls, climbing the stairs to the attic. They propped the windows, levelled his bed. Took up every nook and cranny.

The crunch of gravel disturbed Isabeau's reading. She looked up to see a man carrying a bundle of books. He gripped the knotted twine as though they were fragile treasure, taking care not to let them drag along the ground.

It was her story man. The galleries, the Sundays. But he hadn't come in weeks. She had put him out of her mind. And his companion, she thought, the old fellow. Where was he? They seemed inseparable, and such a lively pair, transforming her quiet Sundays at work. No matter. Here he was again. She felt herself blush.

She watched him circle the pond. Of course he would be a reader, she thought. Naturally all those stories, that imagination, would be fuelled by books. She smiled. How many times had she done as he was doing now, hurrying home after poking around the bookstalls, new purchases under her arm, already planning which one to read first, where they might fit on the shelf?

Please, she whispered, please look this way.

As the story man disappeared under the trees, Isabeau remembered herself. Her hand adjusted the scarf over her cheek.

Henri knew by instinct that his new customer was not a reader. Yet he never said a word as week after week Octavio returned to the stall. What the fellow did with the books was his own affair, Henri thought. He would be glad of the business and the companionship and leave it at that.

While Henri busied himself pulling selections, Octavio would stand for a few minutes, his hat bouncing in his hands, memorizing the portrait of the woman. She reminded him of a picture in his *Arabian Nights*: it was near the beginning of the book, a young woman with flowing black hair and dressed in a jewelled gown. She was whispering in an old man's ear.

When Ocatvio was young, his father would point at the picture. A princess if I ever saw one, he would say. What secrets do you suppose she is telling the king?

The reds gathered in the attic, two or three at a time. Soon stacks of books threatened to block the doorways, as though a bricklayer was using them to slowly close up the apartment. When the walls could hold no more, the floors took over. In turn they began to sag, creaking bitterly under the weight. The blues descended the spiral staircase, half a dozen books to a step. By the time they reached the bottom tread, Octavio had moved on to the greens. These filled the kitchen. Piled under the sink, wedged behind the taps, thrown on top of the cupboards, jammed into the drawers, displayed on the table, three deep along the windowsill. Books in shades of gold followed the slope from bathroom to bedroom. A platform of editions bound in grey cloth raised the bed enough that Octavio needed four thick volumes as a stool to reach the mattress. He removed the mirrored door of the armoire so the purple ones might fit inside. The drawer where he had slept as a baby now barely closed, filled as it was with books the colour of wine. There were ones that flapped in the rafters: Octavio had tied lengths of rope from one beam to the next and hung them open, gently nesting the rope into the gutter of each volume.

Only once did Henri Fournier refuse a purchase. A large book, its worn leather-bound boards the colour of blood oranges, its front decorated with a faded diamond and a pair of exotic slippers.

My apologies, monsieur. I am holding that for someone.

Henri watched the man running his fingers along the spines in the stall. You have been a faithful customer for some time now, he said. For that I am thankful. But I am also curious.

Octavio did not stop his search. About what? he said.

Who, actually. Your father. He had quite an imagination, didn't he? All of France, even the sheep, in mourning I mean.

Octavio nodded.

My grandfather was the same, Henri said. The old man claimed you could tell what a book looked like by closing your eyes and feeling it. I would run my fingers along the spines, as you are now, for hours on end guessing at colours and leathers and linens and foils and embosses. All the while he told me stories. He had a favourite about an Arab who wandered the desert with a library. The fellow would tie stacks of books to the hump of a worn-out camel and the two of them, man and beast, would follow the nomads across the sands. My grandfather would pretend he was this ancient library man, pulling his coat over his head like a shroud and shuffling all over the quay, tugging on an imaginary rope, swatting at invisible flies and cursing an animal only he could see.

Octavio laughed. My father was a baker, he said. The Boulangerie Notre-Dame was his shop. But he always had a story. His best was about how Napoleon had stolen the N from the sign above the bakery's doors. He would crouch on his knees and act like he was the general himself, wobbling on a ladder as he pulled the letter off the sign, then hiding it under a giant hat and sneaking off into the night. The shop is mine now, but the letter is still missing.

I would wager he'd have had a story to tell about my drawings here. What would he have said about the boy and his boat?

Octavio thought for a moment. He might have said—here was a boy who dreamed.

Of what? Henri said.

Of—being the captain of a ship with a hundred black sails. Of voyaging a hundred times around the world: once for every square of canvas. Of standing at a wheel made from the bones of sea monsters, of running down enemy armadas and cannibals in war canoes and murderous pirates. Of crossing the ocean without so much as a puff of wind.

It was Henri's turn to laugh. And the woman? Fortuna?

Octavio looked into the half-hidden face.

My father would have said—she was a—a princess. That she had travelled to one thousand and one strange lands and knew a thousand secrets more. She had seen lands of flying horses and one-eyed monsters, bargained with thieves in caves filled with treasure, met beggar boys rubbing magic lamps, flown on carpets, sung with mermaids, sailed off the edge of the world and lived to tell it all.

Henri watched the man's grey eyes light up. How can I say no to the son of a man who clearly appreciates art? he said. I suppose a few francs are little enough to hear a woman's secrets. Name your price and Fortuna is yours. I have no doubt your father would approve.

A Monday like any other in the bakery. Until a customer glanced up from surveying the morning's selection in the display case.

And who, I wonder, is *that*? they said.

All eyes followed the customer's finger in the direction of the cellar. Above the door, the beer calendar with Our Lady Herself was gone; in her place, the portrait of the woman from Fournier's stall. All heads turned in the direction of Octavio; a few sly grins began to appear.

Has our baker been keeping secrets? a gossip said.

Someone new in your life, monsieur? said another.

Not as much Our Lady and more *your* lady, Octavio?

The clock behind the counter ticked to 9:16. Blind Grenelle entered. He made his way through the crowded shop and stopped in front of the display case. He pointed to two golden brioche sprinkled with a hint of rosemary and looked up at Octavio.

I see we are under new management, he said.

The young woman stumbles as she steps away from the bakery window, fighting for balance, her eyes wide in shock. As unconsciously as breathing, she raises a hand to her face.

On condition, she had said.

She remembers the artist applying his final strokes, rubbing a spot here and there with his thumb. He was moving to reveal the finished portrait when she had stopped him.

I know what I look like, she had said.

As she paid for her sourdough, Madame Lafrouche asked Octavio why he hadn't been to the Louvre lately.

I've been busy with something else, he said, knowing full well that the woman had watched him every Sunday as he returned to the cake-slice with his bundles of books.

You and your father always loved the museum, Madame Lafrouche said.

It has been a while, madame. Have you ever been?

My Alphonse would take me once in a while, a very long time ago now.

It is a grand place, Octavio said.

It would be nice to visit again, Madame Lafrouche said. Bring back a happy memory or two. There was a note of sadness as her voice trailed off.

Why don't you come with me, Octavio said. We could go this Sunday.

Give your book collecting a bit of a break then, Madame Lafrouche said.

Octavio had never seen Madame Lafrouche wink before.

Circular benches rose like islands from the parquet of the Grande Galerie. Here laces could be loosened to free pinched toes, children hushed as they collapsed in bored tantrums, guidebooks thumbed. All with the faces of the gallery looking down from their walls.

Having managed half the length of the gallery, two women had come to rest. Grey and soft in their best Sunday dresses and pinned hats, they folded their hands in their laps and set their sensible shoes firmly on the floor.

They considered the canvas in front of them: a gentleman, his youthful beard rendered in wisps of ginger, posed in a tunic of fine embroidery. In his graceful fingers: a long wooden flute.

You know, said the stouter of the two friends,

someone once said there was no beauty in the flawless.

And where did they say it would be? said the shorter one.

In the flawed, as I remember.

Who said this?

I don't recall. Some great thinker, I imagine.

What's the title of this one then?

Stout read from her guide. *Portrait of the One-Eyed Flautist.*

Painted when?

The book says it is a masterpiece of the Renaissance.

Short cocked her head and asked about the artist.

It doesn't say who painted it, Stout said.

I wouldn't have signed it either. It is quite awful.

He has lovely hands, though. I imagine his would be a very soft touch.

The man is missing an eye, my dear. And the one left behind stares us down as though we were the ones who plucked its mate.

Well I think he is handsome.

Grotesque, you mean. I can barely look.

I wonder how he lost it.

His beauty?

The eye.

———

Octavio and Madame Lafrouche emerged from the flow of visitors moving along the gallery and stopped in front of the flautist.

Here's a fellow I remember, Octavio said.

Very handsome, Madame Lafrouche replied.

I could tell you about him, madame. If you wish. All I need is a word to start me off.

Any word?

Anything will do fine.

Madame Lafrouche looked hard at the flute player. She scanned the young man up and down, settling on the telltale squint where his eye had been.

Wounded, she said.

Octavio furrowed his brow. Very well. Here we have the portrait of a—wounded—soldier. To the delight of his father he has followed in the family trade and become a young lieutenant. His mother is very proud. But handsome uniforms and cavalry charges are not in his dreams. Music is what fills his head. By day he serves his family's hopes and brings honour to their name. Yet by night, alone on the parade ground, he plays his flute for no one but the moon. Then one day during a fencing exercise, to everyone's horror, our young man loses his eye to a poorly aimed foil. Tragedy! His military career is lost forever. But wonder of wonders, he is maimed for life! Even shunned by friends and family, his wildest wishes have at last been—

Excuse us, monsieur.

Octavio and Madame Lafrouche had not noticed the two women sitting behind them on the bench. Short was scowling at them.

You and your friend are blocking our view, monsieur. And what is all this nonsense about the fellow wishing to lose an eye? Who would want such a thing?

Hush, Stout said. It is a charming story. Makes the poor fellow's flaws almost disappear. Please continue, monsieur.

Yes, Madame Lafrouche said. Please continue.

Octavio motioned the three women to huddle in close. And so our handsome flautist plays, he whispered, to this very day. All the happier for his poke in the eye.

It had been so long since she had seen her story man in the museum. In those weeks and months after the first Sunday he did not appear, Isabeau had lurched from worrying that something might have happened, a horrible accident perhaps, to anger that he *had* seen her that day in the watercolour salon, had noticed her scar and was repulsed, to resignation that she would never see him again.

Isabeau watched as he leaned in among the three women. She did not hear what he said to them, but their blushing smiles made her wish she were his audience.

Over their years together, Madame T eventually warmed to Isabeau. Though she maintained a proper distance from her young protégé, and Isabeau knew her own place in the museum's order of things, a shared truth connected them. Madame T could sense Isabeau's silent longing would only grow with the story man's absence. She knew the loss the girl was feeling, had watched Isabeau lose herself in her work, moreover in her books. Madame T knew too well that Isabeau would not find the comfort of her story man in any book. And it broke her heart.

They sat at their tables waiting for Vermeer and Rembrandt. Two obscure works were scheduled to be re-hung in the museum and would need cleaning. The paintings were overdue from storage.

Reading again? Madame T said. Always with your head in a book.

Just finishing, Isabeau said. Would you like to borrow it?

Thank you but no. I don't read much these days.

Books are an amusement for when you are young and in love.

In love? Isabeau said. She quickly closed her book.

I'm sure the museum's gossipers have said I would know nothing of love. But I did fall once. I wasn't much older than you are now.

I was passing Saint-Sulpice on my way home from the museum. I had just started working here. It was April, pouring rain. I stepped into a bookshop to get out of the weather. I dropped my umbrella and suddenly a young man appeared from behind a shelf. He picked up the umbrella and shook off the raindrops. If it is books you like, he said, then I shall have to start reading.

Such a bold move, Isabeau said. An image in her mind, Madame T as a younger woman, took shape. She had been beautiful once, Isabeau thought, angry with herself that she hadn't noticed before.

I suspect that is why I fell for him, Madame said. We talked in the bookshop for quite a while. It was nervous chatter mostly, books we were reading, books we had enjoyed, that sort of thing. As it turned out we had very different tastes.

Which ones did you like? Isabeau said.

I told my gentleman that Victor Hugo was a master and that I had hung on every word of *Les Misérables*.

He said he had wished it were shorter. Now Monsieur Verne, he said, there was a fine writer. When I offered my opinion of such silliness he looked completely deflated. I remember looking in his eyes and being so afraid I had said the wrong thing.

But surely that wasn't the end of it, Isabeau said.

Very much a beginning, Madame T said. We would meet every Saturday. Sometimes at the bookshop, other times at a café on the rue de Rivoli. We came to agree, finally, on Flaubert.

You mentioned a library, Isabeau said.

He told me he had a library, or rather his family did. They had been successful in the wine trade and owned a house in the country. One wing of the house—really it was just a long room, he said—they had turned into a library. His father had named it the Wisdom.

Isabeau raised an eyebrow.

My gentleman told me of the glass cases covering every wall, rising to the ceiling, containing hundreds of books. There were chairs and settees that had their own hinged reading table and lamp. There were padded lapboards, mechanical footstools and adjustable headrests. It was a room devoted to nothing but words, he said. But even his description, in that smooth and soft voice of his, did not do it justice.

You saw the Wisdom? He took you there?

Madame nodded. The floor was covered with a giant carpet, she said, a map of the world. The Mediterranean had been woven with aquamarine threads and across the ocean were knitted greens and yellows of the New World. To the east, brown and grey strands of the Himalayas twisted into the blues and reds of the Orient. North and south were thick white weaves of polar ice.

Madame forced a smile. I asked him to take me away, she said.

My gentleman pointed at the centre of the carpet. A bunch of grapes, stitched in shades of purple and pale green, marked the valley of the Loire and his family home. He suggested I take my shoes off and curl my toes around the grapes. Where would you like to go? he said.

I stepped once or twice to the east. China it is then, he said. I moved west over the mountains. Venice, he said. I took two more steps and stood with one foot on Madrid, the other on Lisbon. Iberia, he said. A few more strides and I had crossed the ocean. And so to America, he said.

I asked him if he knew these places. I know of them, he said. So you have travelled, I said. Not so very far, no. I laughed at him and asked what could he know if he hadn't been anywhere.

He said he knew a place where a stone wall stretched for thousands of miles, concealing a suspicious kingdom from its neighbours. He knew a city where the streets were filled with water and its citizens moved about in boats shaped like black slippers. He knew a land of castles where old men in rusting armour attacked windmills, believing them to be giants. He knew a country covered in trees where warriors painted their bodies so they might drive fear into the hearts of their enemies.

And yet you say you have not travelled, I said. Not so far, he repeated. Then how do you know? With these, he said, waving his hands at the glass cases.

I had no idea madame, Isabeau said. What a wonderful story.

With not much of an ending I'm afraid, Madame T said. My parents had died when I was young and I had been on my own for a long time. A chance meeting in a little bookshop had brought me out of myself. It made me fall in love and took me across the world with no more effort than walking across a room. But it was all such a fragile thing.

Madame T collected herself.

My gentleman would come to the city every weekend. One Saturday morning he did not step off the train. I waited on the platform for hours. He never arrived. For days I wrote to him, asking what had happened, would he be coming next week, had I done something wrong, had he stopped loving me? A month or more passed with no answer. I finally received a letter at the museum, the return address the winery in the Loire. The family's housekeeper had found my name in his effects and was writing to tell me there had been an accident. I haven't been much of a reader since.

I am so sorry, Isabeau said.

Madame T smiled. Don't be, my dear. My paintings keep me company now.

The young woman cannot move.

Horrified at her own face on display, she recognizes someone else. The years of leaning over paintings in the cellar. The Dürers, her David. Her beloved Sofia. For an instant a beautiful woman looks back at her. As though the artist by the boat pond had found her: before her accident, before folding her mother's magazines in the hall of mirrors, before a life draped in a scarf.

She blinks away the vision. Books continue to snow around her. Not knowing where to run, she begins to collect bits of paper off the street, hoping the effort might distract anyone who might look her way.

The baker stands across the street. His knees are shaking; he fights to keep from collapsing. The bundle of books lies at his feet. With no strength left to pick them up, he turns toward the bakery.

He sees a young woman crouched in her summer dress, the loveliest pink, scooping handfuls of paper from the cobblestones, trying to keep her scarf from unravelling. Images rush at him: a woman reading in a garden, a portrait hanging in a bookstall, a face above a cellar door.

He whispers to himself: it is you.

Amid the millions of words written on the subject, the memories of a first blush, the retelling of when-we-met stories, there was no logical explanation. Science and religion offered no biological causes or revealed truths. The snowflake beginning the avalanche remained unseen; the dewdrop that started the deluge could not be identified. Yet there were theories, plenty of those, concerning how one found love.

A boy-god's arrow, some would claim, hitting its mark from behind a billowy cloud. A softening of the brain, others said, the pleasant result of too much wine. The phases of the moon, the alignment of stars, the coming of spring. Forbidden fruits and tempting serpents. The light in a smiling eye, the dimple at the corner of a shy mouth.

Each of these, and countless more, had turned an invisible switch, quickening the pulse and raising the heat in the room. And all without warning: a glimpse of someone, for an instant then gone, as they stood on the opposite platform in the Métro. The bumping of shoulders on a crowded boulevard. A dropped umbrella rescued, shaken dry, returned with a bow. The inexplicable turn of a head in the Tuileries; an overheard story.

One's thoughts were somewhere else when it happened: finding a place—in the attic, under the stairs, squaring a shelf—for the day's purchases; or turning a page in an absorbing chapter; or contemplating the weave of a great kilim map. One minute alone in one's own head, the next staring at someone they had never seen before, or had seen a hundred times, but now with a changed pair of eyes.

What was that? they might have wondered. A twinge in the stomach. A thump, an offbeat skip, a sudden pounding under the breastbone. Had the trees somehow turned greener? Had the breeze, together with the children's boats, stopped moving across the pond?

It might have been the book she was reading, such an aubergine purple. The simple cut of her dress. The slope of her legs, ankles crossed, shoes off, heels resting on the edge of the pond, toes cooling in the breeze. How she held her head, turned down and away, with her face, what he could see of it, inches from the page.

Or the way she looked up from behind her scarf as he passed.

Octavio shuffled across the gravel in the Tuileries: preoccupied as always with keeping the day's bundle from dragging; planning where each book would find its place in the cake-slice. As a gust of wind rippled the boat pond, he turned his head, saw a flash of colour. Peacock blues and greens, a corner of scarf caught in the breeze. A young woman was reading. Looking up from her book, she caught the end of the scarf, pulled it tightly to her cheek and looped it over her shoulder.

It couldn't be her, he thought.

Octavio quickened his pace, his feet stumbling as they knocked against his bundle. Don't run don't run don't run she'll see you don't trip keep your feet the trees into the trees watch out for the branches breathe just breathe it was impossible she couldn't be.

Octavio concealed himself in the shade and pressed

his hand against his heaving chest. He watched as the woman closed her book. She slipped on her shoes, dragged her chair back to the edge of the trees. She checked the knot of her scarf, looked for a moment toward the trees, and walked back to the Louvre.

Octavio followed her. He stopped as she disappeared through the crowds milling around the museum's entrance. Realizing the twine around his books was cutting into his hand, he dropped his bundle. Three or four volumes this day, in shades of tattered brown, came loose and tumbled to the cobbles.

He knew he had seen that face before—obscured in the shadow of a long lock of hair. It was all too unbelievable, he thought. She couldn't be. The woman in the Tuileries could not be the portrait hanging in the bakery. *His* bakery.

The wind in the museum's forecourt seemed suddenly to stop blowing.

For weeks Octavio returned to the shelter of the trees. The woman would appear as the sun reached midday. She would walk to the edge of the trees, find her chair and drag it to the boat pond. Every Sunday the same chair, the same spot. Every Sunday a book.

He needed only one word to imagine a hundred stories: she—

was a dancer; cooling her feet after a morning of twirls and leaps.

was the daughter of a sea captain, remembering her childhood as the toy boats crossed the pond.

was an empress hiding among her subjects, shielding her face with a scarf made from the silk of ten thousand worms. Five thousand green, five thousand blue.

was a teacher, a lover of learning, patient and gentle with her students.

She—was a reader.

He had a library.

It could not continue this way. The clammy palms, the butterfly stomach, the light-headedness. He could not keep watching her and do nothing. He had no idea how—if—he should approach her. He could ask Grenelle for advice but then where would he begin to explain? The fellow would enjoy the story, of that Octavio was certain, but it might be just another fit of imagination to the blind watchmaker. Customers at the bakery would laugh and pump his hand and offer enough contrary advice to make his head spin even faster. And the gossips would have it all over the eighth by the time the morning rush had settled. The thought of that gave Octavio the chills. Then he pictured his father on the bakery's steps.

A beginning then, Emile whispered.

———

Henri Fournier laughed. You are quite mad, my friend.

Octavio said it wasn't funny. Every detail of the drawing that now hung in the bakery he had seared in his mind. He had memorized the woman reading in the Tuileries. They were the same person. There was no mistake.

As you wish, Henri said. Then let us suppose that your brain has not run amok. Does this young woman know you have her portrait?

I don't know. How could she know? Do you think she knows?

Have you introduced yourself?

Should I? How should I? What should I say? What would you say?

Take a breath, my friend. You could ask her what she is reading.

I couldn't do that.

Why not?

She might ask me what I have been reading.

This woman, shall we say your woman, is obviously a lover of books. So you show her your day's purchases. Or you tell her about my stall. I could certainly use the business.

We shall *not* say. She is not *my* woman.

The point is, you may not be a reader like she is, but there's no finer storyteller. Share one of your tales with her.

I cannot speak to her.

Let the story do the talking.

I wouldn't know where to start. Would she give me a word? What word? What if I don't know the word she gives me? What if I can't think of anything?

Henri rolled his eyes. Let us try a different approach, he said. Your woman sits in the same chair, correct?

Every Sunday.

Then leave something for her. Write her a note. Be anonymous if you're going to be so nervous. Be mysterious, like her.

I can't write something. I don't know how—where to begin.

For goodness' sake, a gift then. Flowers are a nice gesture. Or something from your bakery, a token only you could give. Or better yet a book. At least you know she likes those.

She would look up at him, shading her eyes to see who had interrupted her. There would be a moment's pause. She would smile as he asked if she was enjoying her book. I am, she would say, but what are you hiding behind your back? He would bow and hand her his gift. Something from my library, mademoiselle. But I have done nothing to deserve such generosity, monsieur. It made me think of you, he would say. I hope you'll enjoy the pictures, they can tell remarkable stories all by themselves. She would take the parcel and feel the weight of a good book beneath its elegant wrapping paper, her hand lingering on his. Do you have a favourite of these pictures, monsieur? He would nod. Then please join me, she would say. My name is—

Next? Octavio said, catching his hand in the bakery's till.

It was an easy thing to find her chair in the trees. Octavio pulled it to the boat pond and set it as she would have, facing the sun. The precise angle as the back legs dug into the gravel, the exact distance between chair and pond.

The morning promised a warm July day to come. A few children had already taken up their places around the pond. They were preoccupied with their boats, pushing them out, blowing against the little sails, coaxing them to make the great crossing.

He placed the package, wrapped in its iridescent paper, on the woman's chair. He paused, wishing he had the courage to linger under the trees, to see her reaction. To turn and leave contented, knowing that she now knew he had found her.

A small mound of burnt scraps lies in one hand, the other grips the wrapped *Arabian Nights*.

Her accident had become a scar; the scar then a reflex. In turn it had become an instinct. How she might appear to others. Since the day the bandages were removed that instinct had clung to her. She had honed it like a sixth sense: the ability to step away, to look at herself with someone else's eyes.

What they see now is a young woman in a plain dress and scuffed shoes, the poor thing sweating and covered in ash, a beggar in need of a bath and a comb. Tears streak the soot on her face. What once might have been an elegant scarf, now faded, is wrapped in a tangled mess around her head. It hides nothing, enhances nothing, and only makes her appear all the more ridiculous.

Yet she had been beautiful once. In an artist's eyes.

Enough, she thinks.

The sun slid past noon as Isabeau arrived in the Tuileries. She stood by the boat pond, trying to unravel this curiosity. A chair—was it hers?—was already at her customary place. A parcel, beautifully wrapped, lay on the seat. Someone must have forgotten it, she thought. She listened for the sound of footsteps on the gravel, someone running toward her. A mother and son perhaps, their arms waving frantically, eyes wide with worry. You see, Maman? the boy would gasp. I knew someone would find it. Pardon us, mademoiselle, his mother would say. The boy can be such a trial sometimes, but he refused to get on the Métro until we looked.

Isabeau picked up the parcel. She could feel a book inside, a familiar and comfortable weight. The perfect gift, she thought. It would be a shame were someone to lose it. She waited a few minutes more. People strolling around the boat pond paid no attention to her. Finally she sat and pulled her own book from her bag. After a few pages without asterisk or exclamation point or a circled paragraph, Isabeau gave up. She could not concentrate. She looked around the boat pond, then into the trees. No one was coming.

She took the parcel from under her chair and unwrapped it, taking care to not tear the paper. She flipped the book over, read the title. She put it to her nose. There was a vague odour of dust. Isabeau fanned the pages, stopping here and there at a colour plate. Genies, flying carpets, ships teetering at the edge of the world.

She rummaged through the wrapping paper for a card, something that might say who had received such a present, or who had been so generous in the giving. Again she flipped through the book. Inside the back cover she found a tiny, scrawled notation:

F F F From teh the liba library fo of Oct a v oi io ND.
Boula ger ieNoterNotreDame. 8th. Parsi Par ppp Paris.

From one child to another, Isabeau thought. She looked up to see a groundsman raking the gravel near the trees. Their eyes met and Isabeau held her breath, thinking she had been found out, that he knew the book was not hers. The groundsman turned back to his work. Isabeau rewrapped the *Arabian Nights* and slid it into her bag.

That evening as she left the museum, the book nagged at Isabeau. Apart from its scrawled ownership and a few gently curled corners, she had found few flaws. There were no opinions scribbled in margins, no underlined passages. Its pages were firm in their binding; there were no ripped edges where a reader so anxious to learn what happened next had turned the page too quickly. If it had come from someone's library, Isabeau thought, it had rarely been read. At least not the way she would have read it.

Tightening her scarf under her chin, she stepped into a tobacconist's shop and asked for a telephone directory. She slid her finger down column after column of Notre-Dames: accountancies and antiquarians and barbers and barristers and cafés and cheesemongers and dentists and flower shops and jewellers and notaries and opticians and patisseries and pharmacies and tobacconists; cathedrals, chapels, rectories, sisterhoods, benevolent societies and shops offering religious paraphernalia.

There were a few Notre-Dame bakeries, and only one in the eighth. Isabeau fumbled through her bag for a pencil and a scrap of paper. In her neatest handwriting, she copied out the address and hurried out of the shop.

Henri Fournier slouched in front of the bookstall. Though the summer crowds had passed in waves along the quay, there had been only one interested browser. His regular Sunday customer had arrived earlier in the day. He had purchased three books. Henri dared not imagine where he would be were it not for his most curious, painfully shy, but reliably punctual baker.

Henri was dozing off. He needed distraction. The quay had quieted to a few tourists milling near the end of the Pont des Arts. He began pacing in front of the stall, his eyes closed, his hand running along the spines.

He stopped at his grandfather's book. His fingers knew well the front cover's embossed diamond, the pinholes at each corner, the slippers with their curled toes. He had long since memorized the colour of blood oranges.

Henri pulled the book from the shelf. He drew a forefinger across the edge of the pages and found the middle. In one smooth motion he opened the book across his arms. As though it might crumble at the slightest movement, he lowered it to the ground.

Left on the verso right on the recto.

Henri closed his eyes. He lifted his arms out from his shoulders, stretching his fingers as wide as he could.

Lightly, Henri. As weightless as feathers.

Henri curled his toes around the cool smoothness of eggshells. The eggs dissolved into sand and he felt himself sinking. He was at the edge of the sea, the waves eroding the beach around his feet. He wiggled his toes. Another wave slid up the shore. Henri thought he was losing his balance. He opened one eye to catch himself, expecting to see a line of giggling tourists staring at him.

The quay had vanished. The bookstall, the trees, the lamps, the tourists, the bridge, the river, all gone. Henri looked down. His feet were still on the book. But rather than seeing pavement, rooftops were now slowly sliding underneath him. He could see lines of flags and light bulbs strung between the buildings, then remembered the holiday was only days away. With the book lifting him higher, the city fanned out in a great circle, the ribbon of the Seine snaking through a maze of streets and boulevards and gardens. In the distance were hills, church spires, fields, orchards; and then through the clouds, far in the distance, a thin blue smudge of seaside.

Henri laughed and closed his eyes and felt the wind cooling his face.

He did not see a young woman hurry past, then stop suddenly and return to the stall. She rummaged through the selection, ran her hand over an embossing here, inspected an endpaper there, lifted a volume to her face and breathed deeply. She admired the drawing of the boy and his boat. Then, realizing the time, she rushed off in the direction of the Pont des Arts.

She told herself that she would have to return to the bookstall. But where was my head to have not seen it before now? she thought. It was impossible to miss, painted such an interesting shade of green.

She was halfway across the bridge by the time Henri stepped off his grandfather's book and returned it to its place. He adjusted his stool and leaned his back against the stall. A smile spread wide across his face.

Isabeau reached the end of the bridge and turned toward the Tuileries.

Below her, at the river's edge, an old man crouched on his haunches, a ragged carpetbag beside him. In his hands was a square of canvas. He laid it gently on the water and slid it back and forth. The soft colour wash of buildings, the pearl sky, the green bookstalls, a yellow dress walking along the quay, all slowly dissolved, their trails drifting with the current.

As Isabeau passed the boat pond, she resisted the urge to stop. Another Sunday and she would be sitting across the way, content with her reading, looking up from the pages now and then to see if her story man was in sight. She loved those Sundays. But she knew this day's errand was important. Someone was missing their book. And if she didn't return to the Tuileries until later, if it turned out she had missed her story man, then no matter. Next week would come, the pond would be waiting and life would return to its routine.

Isabeau looked under the trees, saw that her chair was where it should be, and hurried on.

The scarf falls away. Lowering her head, the young woman pulls a lock of hair from behind her ear, letting it fall across her cheek. She looks up, one chocolate eye peering out at the baker.

I have something of yours, monsieur.

She holds out the book. From your library, I believe.

The baker reaches for the *Arabian Nights*, then hesitates. My—I—you found it.

The young woman reassures him with a nod. I had hoped for a story, she says.

The baker takes the streak of white in the young

woman's hair and moves it back behind her ear. She watches his eyes: the brightest grey, searching for a beginning. She smiles and ties her hair back with her scarf.

Tell me how we came to this, she says.

ACKNOWLEDGEMENTS

The epigraph is taken from the Penguin Books Great Ideas edition of *The Painter of Modern Life* by Charles Baudelaire, translated by P.E. Charvet, copyright 1972.

References to Emile Notre-Dame's habitual newspaper and its illustrations were inspired by numerous issues of *Le Petit Journal*, published in Paris, on Sundays, between 1890 and 1944.

The article Emile does not read concerning the Seine floods in January 1919 was adapted from an eyewitness account given by H. Warner Allen and reprinted in *The World's Great Events*, published by P. F. Collier & Son in 1950.

Various images in this novel owe a creative debt to the photography of Robert Doisneau (1912–1994) and Henri Cartier-Bresson (1908–2004).

WITH THANKS TO

Laura Barber and Martha Kanya-Forstner. For their hands-across-the-sea madness in taking this novel to heart, their perseverance in the face of lengthening odds that it would ever be delivered, and for their editorial wisdom, grace, and generosity throughout.

Suzanne Brandreth. Tireless guardian, champion and voice of reason.

Shaun Oakey. For his meticulous smoothing of the language and the history. Allyson Latta, for her own editorial fine-toothed comb. Any remaining errors are the author's alone.

Kelly Hill, Terri Nimmo, Erin Cooper, and Carla Kean. For continuing to design, typeset, and produce books of the highest standard.

The houses of Doubleday Canada and Portobello Books (UK). Their support remains steadfast if still somewhat baffling.

And Rebecca Richardson. For listening to the idea that became this novel while lunching *en plein air* in front of Chartres Cathedral. For reading and rereading and rereading and rereading. For suggesting the fire. As ever, TMD.